George MacDonald (10 December 1824 – 18 September 1905) was a Scottish author, poet and Christian minister. He was a pioneering figure in the field of fantasy literature and the mentor of fellow writer Lewis Carroll. In addition to his fairy tales, MacDonald wrote several works on Christian apologetics. His writings have been cited as a major literary influence by many notable authors including W. H. Auden, J. M. Barrie, Lord Dunsany, Hope Mirrlees, Robert E. Howard, L. Frank Baum, T.H. White, Lloyd Alexander, C. S. Lewis, J. R. R. Tolkien, Walter de la Mare, E. Nesbit, Peter S. Beagle, Neil Gaiman and Madeleine L'Engle. C. S. Lewis wrote that he regarded MacDonald as his "master": "Picking up a copy of Phantastes one day at a train-station bookstall, I began to read. A few hours later", said Lewis, "I knew that I had crossed a great frontier." G. K. Chesterton cited The Princess and the Goblin as a book that had "made a difference to my whole existence". (Source: Wikipedia)

Literary works:
Phantastes: A Fairie Romance for Men and Women (1858)
"Cross Purposes" (1862)
"The Second Sight" (1864)
Dealings with the Fairies (1867)
At the Back of the North Wind (1871)
Works of Fancy and Imagination (1871)
The Princess and the Goblin (1872)
The Wise Woman: A Parable (1875)
The Gifts of the Child Christ and Other Tales
The Day Boy and the Night Girl (1882)
The Princess and Curdie (1883)

A DOUBLE STORY
&
CROSS PURPOSES AND THE SHADOWS
George MacDonald

This is a work of fiction. Names, characters, places, and incidents either are the product of the author's imagination or are used fictitiously. Any resemblance to actual persons, living or dead, events, or locales is entirely coincidental.

Copyright © 2019

All rights reserved. No part of this book may be reproduced in any form or by any electronic or mechanical means including information storage and retrieval systems, without permission in writing from the author. The only exception is by a reviewer, who may quote short excerpts in a review.

First Printing: 2019

ISBN 978-93-89508-48-2 (paperback)

ISBN 978-93-89508-49-9 (Hardcover)

Published by Throne Classics

www.throneclassics.com

Contents

A DOUBLE STORY — 9
- I. — 9
- II. — 16
- III. — 24
- IV. — 29
- V. — 35
- VI. — 41
- VII. — 47
- VIII. — 52
- IX. — 57
- X. — 66
- XI. — 71
- XII. — 78
- XIII. — 84
- XIV. — 93

CROSS PURPOSES AND THE SHADOWS — 105
- CROSS PURPOSES — 105
- CHAPTER I. — 105
- CHAPTER II. — 107
- CHAPTER III. — 111
- CHAPTER IV. — 116
- THE SHADOWS — 131
- About Author — 171

A DOUBLE STORY
&
CROSS PURPOSES AND THE SHADOWS

A DOUBLE STORY

I.

There was a certain country where things used to go rather oddly. For instance, you could never tell whether it was going to rain or hail, or whether or not the milk was going to turn sour. It was impossible to say whether the next baby would be a boy, or a girl, or even, after he was a week old, whether he would wake sweet-tempered or cross.

In strict accordance with the peculiar nature of this country of uncertainties, it came to pass one day, that in the midst of a shower of rain that might well be called golden, seeing the sun, shining as it fell, turned all its drops into molten topazes, and every drop was good for a grain of golden corn, or a yellow cowslip, or a buttercup, or a dandelion at least;—while this splendid rain was falling, I say, with a musical patter upon the great leaves of the horse-chestnuts, which hung like Vandyke collars about the necks of the creamy, red-spotted blossoms, and on the leaves of the sycamores, looking as if they had blood in their veins, and on a multitude of flowers, of which some stood up and boldly held out their cups to catch their share, while others cowered down, laughing, under the soft patting blows of the heavy warm drops;—while this lovely rain was washing all the air clean from the motes, and the bad odors, and the poison-seeds that had escaped from their prisons during the long drought;—while it fell, splashing and sparkling, with a hum, and a rush, and a soft clashing—but stop! I am stealing, I find, and not that only, but with clumsy hands spoiling what I steal:—

"O Rain! with your dull twofold sound,

The clash hard by, and the murmur all round:"

—there! take it, Mr. Coleridge;—while, as I was saying, the lovely little rivers whose fountains are the clouds, and which cut their own channels through the air, and make sweet noises rubbing against their banks as they hurry down and down, until at length they are pulled up on a sudden, with a musical plash, in the very heart of an odorous flower, that first gasps and then sighs up a blissful scent, or on the bald head of a stone that never says, Thank you;—while the very sheep felt it blessing them, though it could never reach their skins through the depth of their long wool, and the veriest hedgehog—I mean the one with the longest spikes—came and spiked himself out to impale as many of the drops as he could;—while the rain was thus falling, and the leaves, and the flowers, and the sheep, and the cattle, and the hedgehog, were all busily receiving the golden rain, something happened. It was not a great battle, nor an earthquake, nor a coronation, but something more important than all those put together. A BABY-GIRL WAS BORN; and her father was a king; and her mother was a queen; and her uncles and aunts were princes and princesses; and her first-cousins were dukes and duchesses; and not one of her second-cousins was less than a marquis or marchioness, or of their third-cousins less than an earl or countess: and below a countess they did not care to count. So the little girl was Somebody; and yet for all that, strange to say, the first thing she did was to cry. I told you it was a strange country.

As she grew up, everybody about her did his best to convince her that she was Somebody; and the girl herself was so easily persuaded of it that she quite forgot that anybody had ever told her so, and took it for a fundamental, innate, primary, first-born, self-evident, necessary, and incontrovertible idea and principle that SHE WAS SOMEBODY. And far be it from me to deny it. I will even go so far as to assert that in this odd country there was a huge number of Somebodies. Indeed, it was one of its oddities that every boy and girl in it, was rather too ready to think he or she was Somebody; and the worst of it was that the princess never thought of there being more than one Somebody—and that was herself.

Far away to the north in the same country, on the side of a bleak hill, where a horse-chestnut or a sycamore was never seen, where were no meadows rich with buttercups, only steep, rough, breezy slopes, covered with dry prickly furze and its flowers of red gold, or moister, softer broom with its flowers of yellow gold, and great sweeps of purple heather, mixed with bilberries, and crowberries, and cranberries—no, I am all wrong: there was nothing out yet but a few furze-blossoms; the rest were all waiting behind their doors till they were called; and no full, slow-gliding river with meadow-sweet along its oozy banks, only a little brook here and there, that dashed past without a moment to say, "How do you do?"— there (would you believe it?) while the same cloud that was dropping down golden rain all about the queen's new baby was dashing huge fierce handfuls of hail upon the hills, with such force that they flew spinning off the rocks and stones, went burrowing in the sheep's wool, stung the cheeks and chin of the shepherd with their sharp spiteful little blows, and made his dog wink and whine as they bounded off his hard wise head, and long sagacious nose; only, when they dropped plump down the chimney, and fell hissing in the little fire, they caught it then, for the clever little fire soon sent them up the chimney again, a good deal swollen, and harmless enough for a while, there (what do you think?) among the hailstones, and the heather, and the cold mountain air, another little girl was born, whom the shepherd her father, and the shepherdess her mother, and a good many of her kindred too, thought Somebody. She had not an uncle or an aunt that was less than a shepherd or dairymaid, not a cousin, that was less than a farm-laborer, not a second-cousin that was less than a grocer, and they did not count farther. And yet (would you believe it?) she too cried the very first thing. It WAS an odd country! And, what is still more surprising, the shepherd and shepherdess and the dairymaids and the laborers were not a bit wiser than the king and the queen and the dukes and the marquises and the earls; for they too, one and all, so constantly taught the little woman that she was Somebody, that she also forgot that there were a great many more Somebodies besides herself in the world.

It was, indeed, a peculiar country, very different from ours—so different, that my reader must not be too much surprised when I add the amazing fact, that most of its inhabitants, instead of enjoying the things they had, were always wanting the things they had not, often even the things it was least likely they ever could have. The grown men and women being like this, there is no reason to be further astonished that the Princess Rosamond—the name her parents gave her because it means Rose of the World—should grow up like them, wanting every thing she could and every thing she couldn't have. The things she could have were a great many too many, for her foolish parents always gave her what they could; but still there remained a few things they couldn't give her, for they were only a common king and queen. They could and did give her a lighted candle when she cried for it, and managed by much care that she should not burn her fingers or set her frock on fire; but when she cried for the moon, that they could not give her. They did the worst thing possible, instead, however; for they pretended to do what they could not. They got her a thin disc of brilliantly polished silver, as near the size of the moon as they could agree upon; and, for a time she was delighted.

But, unfortunately, one evening she made the discovery that her moon was a little peculiar, inasmuch as she could not shine in the dark. Her nurse happened to snuff out the candles as she was playing with it; and instantly came a shriek of rage, for her moon had vanished. Presently, through the opening of the curtains, she caught sight of the real moon, far away in the sky, and shining quite calmly, as if she had been there all the time; and her rage increased to such a degree that if it had not passed off in a fit, I do not know what might have come of it.

As she grew up it was still the same, with this difference, that not only must she have every thing, but she got tired of every thing almost as soon as she had it. There was an accumulation of things in her nursery and schoolroom and bedroom that was perfectly appalling. Her mother's wardrobes were almost useless to her, so packed were they with things of which she never took any notice. When she was five years old, they gave her a splendid gold repeater, so close set with diamonds and rubies, that the back was just one crust of gems. In one of her little tempers, as they called her hideously ugly rages, she dashed it against the back of the chimney, after which it never gave a single tick; and some of the diamonds went to the ash-pit. As she grew older still, she became fond of animals, not in a way that brought them much pleasure, or herself much satisfaction. When angry, she would beat them, and try to pull them to pieces, and as soon as she became a little used to them, would neglect them altogether. Then, if they could, they would run away, and she was furious. Some white mice, which she had ceased feeding altogether, did so; and soon the palace was swarming with white mice. Their red eyes might be seen glowing, and their white skins gleaming, in every dark corner; but when it came to the king's finding a nest of them in his second-best crown, he was angry and ordered them to be drowned. The princess heard of it, however, and raised such a clamor, that there they were left until they should run away of themselves; and the poor king had to wear his best crown every day till then. Nothing that was the princess's property, whether she cared for it or not, was to be meddled with.

Of course, as she grew, she grew worse; for she never tried to grow better. She became more and more peevish and fretful every day—dissatisfied not only with what she had, but with all that was around her, and constantly wishing things in general to be different. She found fault with every thing and everybody, and all that happened, and grew more and more disagreeable to every one who had to do with her. At last, when she had nearly killed her nurse, and had all but succeeded in hanging herself, and was miserable from morning to night, her parents thought it time to do something.

A long way from the palace, in the heart of a deep wood of pine-trees, lived a wise woman. In some countries she would have been called a witch; but that would have been a mistake, for she never did any thing wicked, and had more power than any witch could have. As her fame was spread through all the country, the king heard of her; and, thinking she might perhaps be able to suggest something, sent for her. In the dead of the night, lest the princess should know it, the king's messenger brought into the palace a tall woman, muffled from head to foot in a cloak of black cloth. In the presence of both their Majesties, the king, to do her honor, requested her to sit; but she declined, and stood waiting to hear what they had to say. Nor had she to wait long, for almost instantly they began to tell her the dreadful trouble they were in with their only child; first the king talking, then the queen interposing with some yet more dreadful fact, and at times both letting out a torrent of words together, so anxious were they to show the wise woman that their perplexity was real, and their daughter a very terrible one. For a long while there appeared no sign of approaching pause. But the wise woman stood patiently folded in her black cloak, and listened without word or motion. At length silence fell; for they had talked themselves tired, and could not think of any thing more to add to the list of their child's enormities.

After a minute, the wise woman unfolded her arms; and her cloak dropping open in front, disclosed a garment made of a strange stuff, which an old poet who knew her well has thus described:—

"All lilly white, withoutten spot or pride,

That seemd like silke and silver woven neare;

But neither silke nor silver therein did appeare."

"How very badly you have treated her!" said the wise woman. "Poor child!"

"Treated her badly?" gasped the king.

"She is a very wicked child," said the queen; and both glared with indignation.

"Yes, indeed!" returned the wise woman. "She is very naughty indeed, and that she must be made to feel; but it is half your fault too."

"What!" stammered the king. "Haven't we given her every mortal thing she wanted?"

"Surely," said the wise woman: "what else could have all but killed her? You should have given her a few things of the other sort. But you are far too dull to understand me."

"You are very polite," remarked the king, with royal sarcasm on his thin, straight lips.

The wise woman made no answer beyond a deep sigh; and the king and queen sat silent also in their anger, glaring at the wise woman. The silence lasted again for a minute, and then the wise woman folded her cloak around her, and her shining garment vanished like the moon when a great cloud comes over her. Yet another minute passed and the silence endured, for the smouldering wrath of the king and queen choked the channels of their speech. Then the wise woman turned her back on them, and so stood. At this, the rage of the king broke forth; and he cried to the queen, stammering in his fierceness,—

"How should such an old hag as that teach Rosamond good manners? She knows nothing of them herself! Look how she stands!—actually with her back to us."

At the word the wise woman walked from the room. The great folding doors fell to behind her; and the same moment the king and queen were quarrelling like apes as to which of them was to blame for her departure. Before their altercation was over, for it lasted till the early morning, in rushed Rosamond, clutching in her hand a poor little white rabbit, of which she was very fond, and from which, only because it would not come to her when she called it, she was pulling handfuls of fur in the attempt to tear the squealing, pink-eared, red-eyed thing to pieces.

"Rosa, RosaMOND!" cried the queen; whereupon Rosamond threw the rabbit in her mother's face. The king started up in a fury, and ran to seize her. She darted shrieking from the room. The king rushed after her; but, to his amazement, she was nowhere to be seen: the huge hall was empty.—No: just outside the door, close to the threshold, with her back to it, sat the figure of the wise woman, muffled in her dark cloak, with her head bowed over her knees. As the king stood looking at her, she rose slowly, crossed the hall, and walked away down the marble staircase. The king called to her; but she never turned her head, or gave the least sign that she heard him. So quietly did she pass down the wide marble stair, that the king was all but persuaded he had seen only a shadow gliding across the white steps.

For the princess, she was nowhere to be found. The queen went into hysterics; and the rabbit ran away. The king sent out messengers in every direction, but in vain.

In a short time the palace was quiet—as quiet as it used to be before the princess was born. The king and queen cried a little now and then, for the hearts of parents were in that country strangely fashioned; and yet I am afraid the first movement of those very hearts would have been a jump of terror if the ears above them had heard the voice of Rosamond in one of the corridors. As for the rest of the household, they could not have made up a single tear amongst them. They thought, whatever it might be for the princess, it was, for every one else, the best thing that could have happened; and as to what had become of her, if their heads were puzzled, their hearts took no interest in the question. The lord-chancellor alone had an idea about it, but he was far too wise to utter it.

II.

The fact, as is plain, was, that the princess had disappeared in the folds of the wise woman's cloak. When she rushed from the room, the wise woman caught her to her bosom and flung the black garment around her. The princess struggled wildly, for she was in fierce terror, and screamed as loud as choking fright would permit her; but her father, standing in the door, and looking down upon the wise woman, saw never a movement of the cloak, so tight was she held by her captor. He was indeed aware of a most angry crying, which reminded him of his daughter; but it sounded to him so far away, that he took it for the passion of some child in the street, outside the palace-gates. Hence, unchallenged, the wise woman carried the princess down the marble stairs, out at the palace-door, down a great flight of steps outside, across a paved court, through the brazen gates, along half-roused streets where people were opening their shops, through the huge gates of the city, and out into the wide road, vanishing northwards; the princess struggling and screaming all the time, and the wise woman holding her tight. When at length she was too tired to struggle or scream any more, the wise woman unfolded her cloak, and set her down; and the princess saw the light and opened her swollen eyelids. There was nothing in sight that she had ever seen before. City and palace had disappeared. They were upon a wide road going straight on, with a ditch on each side of it, that behind them widened into the great moat surrounding the city. She cast up a terrified look into the wise woman's face, that gazed down upon her gravely and kindly. Now the princess did not in the least understand kindness. She always took it for a sign either of partiality or fear. So when the wise woman looked kindly upon her, she rushed at her, butting with her head like a ram: but the folds of the cloak had closed around the wise woman; and, when the princess ran against it, she found it hard as the cloak of a bronze statue, and fell back upon the road with a great bruise on her head. The wise woman lifted her again, and put her once more under the cloak, where she fell asleep, and where she awoke again only to find that she was still being carried on and on.

When at length the wise woman again stopped and set her down, she saw around her a bright moonlit night, on a wide heath, solitary and houseless. Here she felt more frightened than before; nor was her terror assuaged when, looking up, she saw a stern, immovable countenance, with cold eyes fixedly regarding her. All she knew of the world being derived from nursery-tales, she concluded that the wise woman was an ogress, carrying her home to eat her.

I have already said that the princess was, at this time of her life, such a low-minded creature, that severity had greater influence over her than kindness. She understood terror better far than tenderness. When the wise woman looked at her thus, she fell on her knees, and held up her hands to her, crying,—

"Oh, don't eat me! don't eat me!"

Now this being the best SHE could do, it was a sign she was a low creature. Think of it—to kick at kindness, and kneel from terror. But the sternness on the face of the wise woman came from the same heart and the same feeling as the kindness that had shone from it before. The only thing that could save the princess from her hatefulness, was that she should be made to mind somebody else than her own miserable Somebody.

Without saying a word, the wise woman reached down her hand, took one of Rosamond's, and, lifting her to her feet, led her along through the moonlight. Every now and then a gush of obstinacy would well up in the heart of the princess, and she would give a great ill-tempered tug, and pull her hand away; but then the wise woman would gaze down upon her with such a look, that she instantly sought again the hand she had rejected, in pure terror lest she should be eaten upon the spot. And so they would walk on again; and when the wind blew the folds of the cloak against the princess, she found them soft as her mother's camel-hair shawl.

After a little while the wise woman began to sing to her, and the princess could not help listening; for the soft wind amongst the low dry bushes of the heath, the rustle of their own steps, and the trailing of the wise woman's cloak, were the only sounds beside.

And this is the song she sang:—

> Out in the cold,
>
> With a thin-worn fold
>
> Of withered gold
>
> Around her rolled,

Hangs in the air the weary moon.

> She is old, old, old;
>
> And her bones all cold,
>
> And her tales all told,
>
> And her things all sold,

And she has no breath to croon.

> Like a castaway clout,
>
> She is quite shut out!
>
> She might call and shout,
>
> But no one about

Would ever call back, "Who's there?"

> There is never a hut,
>
> Not a door to shut,
>
> Not a footpath or rut,
>
> Long road or short cut,

Leading to anywhere!

> She is all alone
>
> Like a dog-picked bone,
>
> The poor old crone!

She fain would groan,

But she cannot find the breath.

    She once had a fire;

    But she built it no higher,

    And only sat nigher

    Till she saw it expire;

And now she is cold as death.

    She never will smile

    All the lonesome while.

    Oh the mile after mile,

    And never a stile!

And never a tree or a stone!

    She has not a tear:

    Afar and anear

    It is all so drear,

    But she does not care,

Her heart is as dry as a bone.

    None to come near her!

    No one to cheer her!

    No one to jeer her!

    No one to hear her!

Not a thing to lift and hold!

    She is always awake,

But her heart will not break:

She can only quake,

Shiver, and shake:

The old woman is very cold.

As strange as the song, was the crooning wailing tune that the wise woman sung. At the first note almost, you would have thought she wanted to frighten the princess; and so indeed she did. For when people WILL be naughty, they have to be frightened, and they are not expected to like it. The princess grew angry, pulled her hand away, and cried,—

"YOU are the ugly old woman. I hate you!"

Therewith she stood still, expecting the wise woman to stop also, perhaps coax her to go on: if she did, she was determined not to move a step. But the wise woman never even looked about: she kept walking on steadily, the same pace as before. Little Obstinate thought for certain she would turn; for she regarded herself as much too precious to be left behind. But on and on the wise woman went, until she had vanished away in the dim moonlight. Then all at once the princess perceived that she was left alone with the moon, looking down on her from the height of her loneliness. She was horribly frightened, and began to run after the wise woman, calling aloud. But the song she had just heard came back to the sound of her own running feet,—

All all alone,

Like a dog-picked bone!

and again,—

She might call and shout,

And no one about

Would ever call back, "Who's there?"

and she screamed as she ran. How she wished she knew the old woman's name, that she might call it after her through the moonlight!

But the wise woman had, in truth, heard the first sound of her running feet, and stopped and turned, waiting. What with running and crying, however, and a fall or two as she ran, the princess never saw her until she fell right into her arms—and the same moment into a fresh rage; for as soon as any trouble was over the princess was always ready to begin another. The wise woman therefore pushed her away, and walked on; while the princess ran scolding and storming after her. She had to run till, from very fatigue, her rudeness ceased. Her heart gave way; she burst into tears, and ran on silently weeping.

A minute more and the wise woman stooped, and lifting her in her arms, folded her cloak around her. Instantly she fell asleep, and slept as soft and as soundly as if she had been in her own bed. She slept till the moon went down; she slept till the sun rose up; she slept till he climbed the topmost sky; she slept till he went down again, and the poor old moon came peaking and peering out once more: and all that time the wise woman went walking on and on very fast. And now they had reached a spot where a few fir-trees came to meet them through the moonlight.

At the same time the princess awaked, and popping her head out between the folds of the wise woman's cloak—a very ugly little owlet she looked—saw that they were entering the wood. Now there is something awful about every wood, especially in the moonlight; and perhaps a fir-wood is more awful than other woods. For one thing, it lets a little more light through, rendering the darkness a little more visible, as it were; and then the trees go stretching away up towards the moon, and look as if they cared nothing about the creatures below them—not like the broad trees with soft wide leaves that, in the darkness even, look sheltering. So the princess is not to be blamed that she was very much frightened. She is hardly to be blamed either that, assured the wise woman was an ogress carrying her to her castle to eat her up, she began again to kick and scream violently, as those of my readers who are of the same sort as herself will consider the right and natural thing to do. The wrong in her was this—that she had led such a bad life, that she did not know a good woman when she saw her; took her for one like herself, even after she had slept in her arms.

Immediately the wise woman set her down, and, walking on, within a few paces vanished among the trees. Then the cries of the princess rent the air, but the fir-trees never heeded her; not one of their hard little needles gave a single shiver for all the noise she made. But there were creatures in the forest who were soon quite as much interested in her cries as the fir-trees were indifferent to them. They began to hearken and howl and snuff about, and run hither and thither, and grin with their white teeth, and light up the green lamps in their eyes. In a minute or two a whole army of wolves and hyenas were rushing from all quarters through the pillar like stems of the fir-trees, to the place where she stood calling them, without knowing it. The noise she made herself, however, prevented her from hearing either their howls or the soft pattering of their many trampling feet as they bounded over the fallen fir needles and cones.

One huge old wolf had outsped the rest—not that he could run faster, but that from experience he could more exactly judge whence the cries came, and as he shot through the wood, she caught sight at last of his lamping eyes coming swiftly nearer and nearer. Terror silenced her. She stood with her mouth open, as if she were going to eat the wolf, but she had no breath to scream with, and her tongue curled up in her mouth like a withered and frozen leaf. She could do nothing but stare at the coming monster. And now he was taking a few shorter bounds, measuring the distance for the one final leap that should bring him upon her, when out stepped the wise woman from behind the very tree by which she had set the princess down, caught the wolf by the throat half-way in his last spring, shook him once, and threw him from her dead. Then she turned towards the princess, who flung herself into her arms, and was instantly lapped in the folds of her cloak.

But now the huge army of wolves and hyenas had rushed like a sea around them, whose waves leaped with hoarse roar and hollow yell up against the wise woman. But she, like a strong stately vessel, moved unhurt through the midst of them. Ever as they leaped against her cloak, they dropped and slunk away back through the crowd. Others ever succeeded, and ever in their turn fell, and drew back confounded. For some time she walked on attended and assailed on all sides by the howling pack. Suddenly they turned and swept away, vanishing in the depths of the forest. She neither slackened nor hastened her step, but went walking on as before.

In a little while she unfolded her cloak, and let the princess look out. The firs had ceased; and they were on a lofty height of moorland, stony and bare and dry, with tufts of heather and a few small plants here and there. About the heath, on every side, lay the forest, looking in the moonlight like a cloud; and above the forest, like the shaven crown of a monk, rose the bare moor over which they were walking. Presently, a little way in front of them, the princess espied a whitewashed cottage, gleaming in the moon. As they came nearer, she saw that the roof was covered with thatch, over which the moss had grown green. It was a very simple, humble place, not in the least terrible to look at, and yet, as soon as she saw it, her fear again awoke, and always, as soon as her fear awoke, the trust of the princess fell into a dead sleep. Foolish and useless as she might by this time have known it, she once more began kicking and screaming, whereupon, yet once more, the wise woman set her down on the heath, a few yards from the back of the cottage, and saying only, "No one ever gets into my house who does not knock at the door, and ask to come in," disappeared round the corner of the cottage, leaving the princess alone with the moon—two white faces in the cone of the night.

III.

The moon stared at the princess, and the princess stared at the moon; but the moon had the best of it, and the princess began to cry. And now the question was between the moon and the cottage. The princess thought she knew the worst of the moon, and she knew nothing at all about the cottage, therefore she would stay with the moon. Strange, was it not, that she should have been so long with the wise woman, and yet know NOTHING about that cottage? As for the moon, she did not by any means know the worst of her, or even, that, if she were to fall asleep where she could find her, the old witch would certainly do her best to twist her face.

But she had scarcely sat a moment longer before she was assailed by all sorts of fresh fears. First of all, the soft wind blowing gently through the dry stalks of the heather and its thousands of little bells raised a sweet rustling, which the princess took for the hissing of serpents, for you know she had been naughty for so long that she could not in a great many things tell the good from the bad. Then nobody could deny that there, all round about the heath, like a ring of darkness, lay the gloomy fir-wood, and the princess knew what it was full of, and every now and then she thought she heard the howling of its wolves and hyenas. And who could tell but some of them might break from their covert and sweep like a shadow across the heath? Indeed, it was not once nor twice that for a moment she was fully persuaded she saw a great beast coming leaping and bounding through the moonlight to have her all to himself. She did not know that not a single evil creature dared set foot on that heath, or that, if one should do so, it would that instant wither up and cease. If an army of them had rushed to invade it, it would have melted away on the edge of it, and ceased like a dying wave.—She even imagined that the moon was slowly coming nearer and nearer down the sky to take her and freeze her to death in her arms. The wise woman, too, she felt sure, although her cottage looked asleep, was watching her at some little window. In this, however, she would have been quite right, if she had only imagined enough—namely, that the wise woman was watching OVER her from the little window. But after all, somehow, the thought of the wise woman was less frightful than that of any of her other terrors, and at length she began to wonder whether it might not turn out that she was no ogress, but only a rude, ill-bred, tyrannical, yet on the whole not altogether ill-meaning person. Hardly had the possibility arisen in her mind, before she was on her feet: if the woman was any thing short of an ogress, her cottage must be better than that horrible loneliness, with nothing in all the world but a stare; and even an ogress had at least the shape and look of a human being.

She darted round the end of the cottage to find the front. But, to her surprise, she came only to another back, for no door was to be seen. She tried the farther end, but still no door. She must have passed it as she ran—but no—neither in gable nor in side was any to be found.

A cottage without a door!—she rushed at it in a rage and kicked at the wall with her feet. But the wall was hard as iron, and hurt her sadly through her gay silken slippers. She threw herself on the heath, which came up to the walls of the cottage on every side, and roared and screamed with rage. Suddenly, however, she remembered how her screaming had brought the horde of wolves and hyenas about her in the forest, and, ceasing at once, lay still, gazing yet again at the moon. And then came the thought of her parents in the palace at home. In her mind's eye she saw her mother sitting at her embroidery with the tears dropping upon it, and her father staring into the fire as if he were looking for her in its glowing caverns. It is true that if they had both been in tears by her side because of her naughtiness, she would not have cared a straw; but now her own forlorn condition somehow helped her to understand their grief at having lost her, and not only a great longing to be back in her comfortable home, but a feeble flutter of genuine love for her parents awoke in her heart as well, and she burst into real tears—soft, mournful tears—very different from those of rage and disappointment to which she was so much used. And another very remarkable thing was that the moment she began to love her father and mother, she began to wish to see the wise woman again. The idea of her being an ogress vanished utterly, and she thought of her only as one to take her in from the moon, and the loneliness, and the terrors of the forest-haunted heath, and hide her in a cottage with not even a door for the horrid wolves to howl against.

But the old woman—as the princess called her, not knowing that her real name was the Wise Woman—had told her that she must knock at the door: how was she to do that when there was no door? But again she bethought herself—that, if she could not do all she was told, she could, at least, do a part of it: if she could not knock at the door, she could at least knock—say on the wall, for there was nothing else to knock upon—and perhaps the old woman would hear her, and lift her in by some window. Thereupon, she rose at once to her feet, and picking up a stone, began to knock on the wall with it. A loud noise was the result, and she found she was knocking on the very door itself. For a moment she feared the old woman would be offended, but the next, there came a voice, saying,

"Who is there?"

The princess answered,

"Please, old woman, I did not mean to knock so loud."

To this there came no reply.

Then the princess knocked again, this time with her knuckles, and the voice came again, saying,

"Who is there?"

And the princess answered,

"Rosamond."

Then a second time there was silence. But the princess soon ventured to knock a third time.

"What do you want?" said the voice.

"Oh, please, let me in!" said the princess.

"The moon will keep staring at me; and I hear the wolves in the wood."

Then the door opened, and the princess entered. She looked all around, but saw nothing of the wise woman.

It was a single bare little room, with a white deal table, and a few old wooden chairs, a fire of fir-wood on the hearth, the smoke of which smelt sweet, and a patch of thick-growing heath in one corner. Poor as it was, compared to the grand place Rosamond had left, she felt no little satisfaction as she shut the door, and looked around her. And what with the sufferings and terrors she had left outside, the new kind of tears she had shed, the love she had begun to feel for her parents, and the trust she had begun to place in the wise woman, it seemed to her as if her soul had grown larger of a sudden, and she had left the days of her childishness and naughtiness far behind her. People are so ready to think themselves changed when it is only their mood that is changed! Those who are good-tempered because it is a fine day, will be ill-tempered when it rains: their selves are just the same both days; only in the one case, the fine weather has got into them, in the other the rainy. Rosamond, as she sat warming herself by the glow of the peat-fire, turning over in her mind all that had passed, and feeling how pleasant the change in her feelings was, began by degrees to think how very good she had grown, and how very good she was to have grown good, and how extremely good she must always have been that she was able to grow so very good as she now felt she had grown; and she became so absorbed in her self-admiration as never to notice either that the fire was dying, or that a heap of fir-cones lay in a corner near it. Suddenly, a great wind came roaring down the chimney, and scattered the ashes about the floor; a tremendous rain followed, and fell hissing on the embers; the moon was swallowed up, and there was darkness all about her. Then a flash of lightning, followed by a peal of thunder, so terrified the princess, that she cried aloud for the old woman, but there came no answer to her cry.

Then in her terror the princess grew angry, and saying to herself, "She must be somewhere in the place, else who was there to open the door to me?" began to shout and yell, and call the wise woman all the bad names she had been in the habit of throwing at her nurses. But there came not a single sound in reply.

Strange to say, the princess never thought of telling herself now how naughty she was, though that would surely have been reasonable. On the contrary, she thought she had a perfect right to be angry, for was she not most desperately ill used—and a princess too? But the wind howled on, and the rain kept pouring down the chimney, and every now and then the lightning burst out, and the thunder rushed after it, as if the great lumbering sound could ever think to catch up with the swift light!

At length the princess had again grown so angry, frightened, and miserable, all together, that she jumped up and hurried about the cottage with outstretched arms, trying to find the wise woman. But being in a bad temper always makes people stupid, and presently she struck her forehead such a blow against something—she thought herself it felt like the old woman's cloak—that she fell back—not on the floor, though, but on the patch of heather, which felt as soft and pleasant as any bed in the palace. There, worn out with weeping and rage, she soon fell fast asleep.

She dreamed that she was the old cold woman up in the sky, with no home and no friends, and no nothing at all, not even a pocket; wandering, wandering forever, over a desert of blue sand, never to get to anywhere, and never to lie down or die. It was no use stopping to look about her, for what had she to do but forever look about her as she went on and on and on—never seeing any thing, and never expecting to see any thing! The only shadow of a hope she had was, that she might by slow degrees grow thinner and thinner, until at last she wore away to nothing at all; only alas! she could not detect the least sign that she had yet begun to grow thinner. The hopelessness grew at length so unendurable that she woke with a start. Seeing the face of the wise woman bending over her, she threw her arms around her neck and held up her mouth to be kissed. And the kiss of the wise woman was like the rose-gardens of Damascus.

IV.

The wise woman lifted her tenderly, and washed and dressed her far more carefully than even her nurse. Then she set her down by the fire, and prepared her breakfast. The princess was very hungry, and the bread and milk as good as it could be, so that she thought she had never in her life eaten any thing nicer. Nevertheless, as soon as she began to have enough, she said to herself,—

"Ha! I see how it is! The old woman wants to fatten me! That is why she gives me such nice creamy milk. She doesn't kill me now because she's going to kill me then! She IS an ogress, after all!"

Thereupon she laid down her spoon, and would not eat another mouthful—only followed the basin with longing looks, as the wise woman carried it away.

When she stopped eating, her hostess knew exactly what she was thinking; but it was one thing to understand the princess, and quite another to make the princess understand her: that would require time. For the present she took no notice, but went about the affairs of the house, sweeping the floor, brushing down the cobwebs, cleaning the hearth, dusting the table and chairs, and watering the bed to keep it fresh and alive—for she never had more than one guest at a time, and never would allow that guest to go to sleep upon any thing that had no life in it. All the time she was thus busied, she spoke not a word to the princess, which, with the princess, went to confirm her notion of her purposes. But whatever she might have said would have been only perverted by the princess into yet stronger proof of her evil designs, for a fancy in her own head would outweigh any multitude of facts in another's. She kept staring at the fire, and never looked round to see what the wise woman might be doing.

By and by she came close up to the back of her chair, and said,

"Rosamond!"

But the princess had fallen into one of her sulky moods, and shut herself up with her own ugly Somebody; so she never looked round or even answered the wise woman.

"Rosamond," she repeated, "I am going out. If you are a good girl, that is, if you do as I tell you, I will carry you back to your father and mother the moment I return."

The princess did not take the least notice.

"Look at me, Rosamond," said the wise woman.

But Rosamond never moved—never even shrugged her shoulders—perhaps because they were already up to her ears, and could go no farther.

"I want to help you to do what I tell you," said the wise woman. "Look at me."

Still Rosamond was motionless and silent, saying only to herself,

"I know what she's after! She wants to show me her horrid teeth. But I won't look. I'm not going to be frightened out of my senses to please her."

"You had better look, Rosamond. Have you forgotten how you kissed me this morning?"

But Rosamond now regarded that little throb of affection as a momentary weakness into which the deceitful ogress had betrayed her, and almost despised herself for it. She was one of those who the more they are coaxed are the more disagreeable. For such, the wise woman had an awful punishment, but she remembered that the princess had been very ill brought up, and therefore wished to try her with all gentleness first.

She stood silent for a moment, to see what effect her words might have. But Rosamond only said to herself,—

"She wants to fatten and eat me."

And it was such a little while since she had looked into the wise woman's loving eyes, thrown her arms round her neck, and kissed her!

"Well," said the wise woman gently, after pausing as long as it seemed possible she might bethink herself, "I must tell you then without; only whoever listens with her back turned, listens but half, and gets but half the help."

"She wants to fatten me," said the princess.

"You must keep the cottage tidy while I am out. When I come back, I must see the fire bright, the hearth swept, and the kettle boiling; no dust on the table or chairs, the windows clear, the floor clean, and the heather in blossom—which last comes of sprinkling it with water three times a day. When you are hungry, put your hand into that hole in the wall, and you will find a meal."

"She wants to fatten me," said the princess.

"But on no account leave the house till I come back," continued the wise woman, "or you will grievously repent it. Remember what you have already gone through to reach it. Dangers lie all around this cottage of mine; but inside, it is the safest place—in fact the only quite safe place in all the country."

"She means to eat me," said the princess, "and therefore wants to frighten me from running away."

She heard the voice no more. Then, suddenly startled at the thought of being alone, she looked hastily over her shoulder. The cottage was indeed empty of all visible life. It was soundless, too: there was not even a ticking clock or a flapping flame. The fire burned still and smouldering-wise; but it was all the company she had, and she turned again to stare into it.

Soon she began to grow weary of having nothing to do. Then she remembered that the old woman, as she called her, had told her to keep the house tidy.

"The miserable little pig-sty!" she said. "Where's the use of keeping such a hovel clean!"

But in truth she would have been glad of the employment, only just because she had been told to do it, she was unwilling; for there ARE people—however unlikely it may seem—who object to doing a thing for no other reason than that it is required of them.

"I am a princess," she said, "and it is very improper to ask me to do such a thing."

She might have judged it quite as suitable for a princess to sweep away the dust as to sit the centre of a world of dirt. But just because she ought, she wouldn't. Perhaps she feared that if she gave in to doing her duty once, she might have to do it always—which was true enough—for that was the very thing for which she had been specially born.

Unable, however, to feel quite comfortable in the resolve to neglect it, she said to herself, "I'm sure there's time enough for such a nasty job as that!" and sat on, watching the fire as it burned away, the glowing red casting off white flakes, and sinking lower and lower on the hearth.

By and by, merely for want of something to do, she would see what the old woman had left for her in the hole of the wall. But when she put in her hand she found nothing there, except the dust which she ought by this time to have wiped away. Never reflecting that the wise woman had told her she would find food there WHEN SHE WAS HUNGRY, she flew into one of her furies, calling her a cheat, and a thief, and a liar, and an ugly old witch, and an ogress, and I do not know how many wicked names besides. She raged until she was quite exhausted, and then fell fast asleep on her chair. When she awoke the fire was out.

By this time she was hungry; but without looking in the hole, she began again to storm at the wise woman, in which labor she would no doubt have once more exhausted herself, had not something white caught her eye: it was the corner of a napkin hanging from the hole in the wall. She bounded to it, and there was a dinner for her of something strangely good—one of her favorite dishes, only better than she had ever tasted it before. This might surely have at least changed her mood towards the wise woman; but she only grumbled to herself that it was as it ought to be, ate up the food, and lay down on the bed, never thinking of fire, or dust, or water for the heather.

The wind began to moan about the cottage, and grew louder and louder, till a great gust came down the chimney, and again scattered the white ashes all over the place. But the princess was by this time fast asleep, and never woke till the wind had sunk to silence. One of the consequences, however, of sleeping when one ought to be awake is waking when one ought to be asleep; and the princess awoke in the black midnight, and found enough to keep her awake. For although the wind had fallen, there was a far more terrible howling than that of the wildest wind all about the cottage. Nor was the howling all; the air was full of strange cries; and everywhere she heard the noise of claws scratching against the house, which seemed all doors and windows, so crowded were the sounds, and from so many directions. All the night long she lay half swooning, yet listening to the hideous noises. But with the first glimmer of morning they ceased.

Then she said to herself, "How fortunate it was that I woke! They would have eaten me up if I had been asleep." The miserable little wretch actually talked as if she had kept them out! If she had done her work in the day, she would have slept through the terrors of the darkness, and awaked fearless; whereas now, she had in the storehouse of her heart a whole harvest of agonies, reaped from the dun fields of the night!

They were neither wolves nor hyenas which had caused her such dismay, but creatures of the air, more frightful still, which, as soon as the smoke of the burning fir-wood ceased to spread itself abroad, and the sun was a sufficient distance down the sky, and the lone cold woman was out, came flying and howling about the cottage, trying to get in at every door and window. Down the chimney they would have got, but that at the heart of the fire there always lay a certain fir-cone, which looked like solid gold red-hot, and which, although it might easily get covered up with ashes, so as to be quite invisible, was continually in a glow fit to kindle all the fir-cones in the world; this it was which had kept the horrible birds—some say they have a claw at the tip of every wing-feather—from tearing the poor naughty princess to pieces, and gobbling her up.

When she rose and looked about her, she was dismayed to see what a state the cottage was in. The fire was out, and the windows were all dim with the wings and claws of the dirty birds, while the bed from which she had just risen was brown and withered, and half its purple bells had fallen. But she consoled herself that she could set all to rights in a few minutes—only she must breakfast first. And, sure enough, there was a basin of the delicious bread and milk ready for her in the hole of the wall!

After she had eaten it, she felt comfortable, and sat for a long time building castles in the air—till she was actually hungry again, without having done an atom of work. She ate again, and was idle again, and ate again. Then it grew dark, and she went trembling to bed, for now she remembered the horrors of the last night. This time she never slept at all, but spent the long hours in grievous terror, for the noises were worse than before. She vowed she would not pass another night in such a hateful haunted old shed for all the ugly women, witches, and ogresses in the wide world. In the morning, however, she fell asleep, and slept late.

Breakfast was of course her first thought, after which she could not avoid that of work. It made her very miserable, but she feared the consequences of being found with it undone. A few minutes before noon, she actually got up, took her pinafore for a duster, and proceeded to dust the table. But the wood-ashes flew about so, that it seemed useless to attempt getting rid of them, and she sat down again to think what was to be done. But there is very little indeed to be done when we will not do that which we have to do.

Her first thought now was to run away at once while the sun was high, and get through the forest before night came on. She fancied she could easily go back the way she had come, and get home to her father's palace. But not the most experienced traveller in the world can ever go back the way the wise woman has brought him.

She got up and went to the door. It was locked! What could the old woman have meant by telling her not to leave the cottage? She was indignant.

The wise woman had meant to make it difficult, but not impossible. Before the princess, however, could find the way out, she heard a hand at the door, and darted in terror behind it. The wise woman opened it, and, leaving it open, walked straight to the hearth. Rosamond immediately slid out, ran a little way, and then laid herself down in the long heather.

V.

The wise woman walked straight up to the hearth, looked at the fire, looked at the bed, glanced round the room, and went up to the table. When she saw the one streak in the thick dust which the princess had left there, a smile, half sad, half pleased, like the sun peeping through a cloud on a rainy day in spring, gleamed over her face. She went at once to the door, and called in a loud voice,

"Rosamond, come to me."

All the wolves and hyenas, fast asleep in the wood, heard her voice, and shivered in their dreams. No wonder then that the princess trembled, and found herself compelled, she could not understand how, to obey the summons. She rose, like the guilty thing she felt, forsook of herself the hiding-place she had chosen, and walked slowly back to the cottage she had left full of the signs of her shame. When she entered, she saw the wise woman on her knees, building up the fire with fir-cones. Already the flame was climbing through the heap in all directions, crackling gently, and sending a sweet aromatic odor through the dusty cottage.

"That is my part of the work," she said, rising. "Now you do yours. But first let me remind you that if you had not put it off, you would have found it not only far easier, but by and by quite pleasant work, much more pleasant than you can imagine now; nor would you have found the time go wearily: you would neither have slept in the day and let the fire out, nor waked at night and heard the howling of the beast-birds. More than all, you would have been glad to see me when I came back; and would have leaped into my arms instead of standing there, looking so ugly and foolish."

As she spoke, suddenly she held up before the princess a tiny mirror, so clear that nobody looking into it could tell what it was made of, or even see it at all—only the thing reflected in it. Rosamond saw a child with dirty fat cheeks, greedy mouth, cowardly eyes—which, not daring to look forward, seemed trying to hide behind an impertinent nose—stooping shoulders, tangled hair, tattered clothes, and smears and stains everywhere. That was what she had made herself. And to tell the truth, she was shocked at the sight, and immediately began, in her dirty heart, to lay the blame on the wise woman, because she had taken her away from her nurses and her fine clothes; while all the time she knew well enough that, close by the heather-bed, was the loveliest little well, just big enough to wash in, the water of which was always springing fresh from the ground, and running away through the wall. Beside it lay the whitest of linen towels, with a comb made of mother-of-pearl, and a brush of fir-needles, any one of which she had been far too lazy to use. She dashed the glass out of the wise woman's hand, and there it lay, broken into a thousand pieces!

Without a word, the wise woman stooped, and gathered the fragments—did not leave searching until she had gathered the last atom, and she laid them all carefully, one by one, in the fire, now blazing high on the hearth. Then she stood up and looked at the princess, who had been watching her sulkily.

"Rosamond," she said, with a countenance awful in its sternness, "until you have cleansed this room—"

"She calls it a room!" sneered the princess to herself.

"You shall have no morsel to eat. You may drink of the well, but nothing else you shall have. When the work I set you is done, you will find food in the same place as before. I am going from home again; and again I warn you not to leave the house."

"She calls it a house!—It's a good thing she's going out of it anyhow!" said the princess, turning her back for mere rudeness, for she was one who, even if she liked a thing before, would dislike it the moment any person in authority over her desired her to do it.

When she looked again, the wise woman had vanished.

Thereupon the princess ran at once to the door, and tried to open it; but open it would not. She searched on all sides, but could discover no way of getting out. The windows would not open—at least she could not open them;

and the only outlet seemed the chimney, which she was afraid to try because of the fire, which looked angry, she thought, and shot out green flames when she went near it. So she sat down to consider. One may well wonder what room for consideration there was—with all her work lying undone behind her. She sat thus, however, considering, as she called it, until hunger began to sting her, when she jumped up and put her hand as usual in the hole of the wall: there was nothing there. She fell straight into one of her stupid rages; but neither her hunger nor the hole in the wall heeded her rage. Then, in a burst of self-pity, she fell a-weeping, but neither the hunger nor the hole cared for her tears. The darkness began to come on, and her hunger grew and grew, and the terror of the wild noises of the last night invaded her. Then she began to feel cold, and saw that the fire was dying. She darted to the heap of cones, and fed it. It blazed up cheerily, and she was comforted a little. Then she thought with herself it would surely be better to give in so far, and do a little work, than die of hunger. So catching up a duster, she began upon the table. The dust flew about and nearly choked her. She ran to the well to drink, and was refreshed and encouraged. Perceiving now that it was a tedious plan to wipe the dust from the table on to the floor, whence it would have all to be swept up again, she got a wooden platter, wiped the dust into that, carried it to the fire, and threw it in. But all the time she was getting more and more hungry and, although she tried the hole again and again, it was only to become more and more certain that work she must if she would eat.

At length all the furniture was dusted, and she began to sweep the floor, which happily, she thought of sprinkling with water, as from the window she had seen them do to the marble court of the palace. That swept, she rushed again to the hole—but still no food! She was on the verge of another rage, when the thought came that she might have forgotten something. To her dismay she found that table and chairs and every thing was again covered with dust—not so badly as before, however. Again she set to work, driven by hunger, and drawn by the hope of eating, and yet again, after a second careful wiping, sought the hole. But no! nothing was there for her! What could it mean?

Her asking this question was a sign of progress: it showed that she expected the wise woman to keep her word. Then she bethought her that she had forgotten the household utensils, and the dishes and plates, some of which wanted to be washed as well as dusted.

Faint with hunger, she set to work yet again. One thing made her think of another, until at length she had cleaned every thing she could think of. Now surely she must find some food in the hole!

When this time also there was nothing, she began once more to abuse the wise woman as false and treacherous;—but ah! there was the bed unwatered! That was soon amended.—Still no supper! Ah! there was the hearth unswept, and the fire wanted making up!—Still no supper! What else could there be? She was at her wits' end, and in very weariness, not laziness this time, sat down and gazed into the fire. There, as she gazed, she spied something brilliant,—shining even, in the midst of the fire: it was the little mirror all whole again; but little she knew that the dust which she had thrown into the fire had helped to heal it. She drew it out carefully, and, looking into it, saw, not indeed the ugly creature she had seen there before, but still a very dirty little animal; whereupon she hurried to the well, took off her clothes, plunged into it, and washed herself clean. Then she brushed and combed her hair, made her clothes as tidy as might be, and ran to the hole in the wall: there was a huge basin of bread and milk!

Never had she eaten any thing with half the relish! Alas! however, when she had finished, she did not wash the basin, but left it as it was, revealing how entirely all the rest had been done only from hunger. Then she threw herself on the heather, and was fast asleep in a moment. Never an evil bird came near her all that night, nor had she so much as one troubled dream.

In the morning as she lay awake before getting up, she spied what seemed a door behind the tall eight-day clock that stood silent in the corner.

"Ah!" she thought, "that must be the way out!" and got up instantly. The first thing she did, however, was to go to the hole in the wall. Nothing was there.

"Well, I am hardly used!" she cried aloud. "All that cleaning for the cross old woman yesterday, and this for my trouble,—nothing for breakfast! Not even a crust of bread! Does Mistress Ogress fancy a princess will bear that?"

The poor foolish creature seemed to think that the work of one day ought to serve for the next day too! But that is nowhere the way in the whole universe. How could there be a universe in that case? And even she never dreamed of applying the same rule to her breakfast.

"How good I was all yesterday!" she said, "and how hungry and ill used I am to-day!"

But she would NOT be a slave, and do over again to-day what she had done only last night! SHE didn't care about her breakfast! She might have it no doubt if she dusted all the wretched place again, but she was not going to do that—at least, without seeing first what lay behind the clock!

Off she darted, and putting her hand behind the clock found the latch of a door. It lifted, and the door opened a little way. By squeezing hard, she managed to get behind the clock, and so through the door. But how she stared, when instead of the open heath, she found herself on the marble floor of a large and stately room, lighted only from above. Its walls were strengthened by pilasters, and in every space between was a large picture, from cornice to floor. She did not know what to make of it. Surely she had run all round the cottage, and certainly had seen nothing of this size near it! She forgot that she had also run round what she took for a hay-mow, a peat-stack, and several other things which looked of no consequence in the moonlight.

"So, then," she cried, "the old woman IS a cheat! I believe she's an ogress, after all, and lives in a palace—though she pretends it's only a cottage, to keep people from suspecting that she eats good little children like me!"

Had the princess been tolerably tractable, she would, by this time, have known a good deal about the wise woman's beautiful house, whereas she had never till now got farther than the porch. Neither was she at all in its innermost places now.

But, king's daughter as she was, she was not a little daunted when, stepping forward from the recess of the door, she saw what a great lordly hall it was. She dared hardly look to the other end, it seemed so far off: so she began to gaze at the things near her, and the pictures first of all, for she had a great liking for pictures. One in particular attracted her attention. She came back to it several times, and at length stood absorbed in it.

A blue summer sky, with white fleecy clouds floating beneath it, hung over a hill green to the very top, and alive with streams darting down its sides toward the valley below. On the face of the hill strayed a flock of sheep feeding, attended by a shepherd and two dogs. A little way apart, a girl stood with bare feet in a brook, building across it a bridge of rough stones. The wind was blowing her hair back from her rosy face. A lamb was feeding close beside her; and a sheepdog was trying to reach her hand to lick it.

"Oh, how I wish I were that little girl!" said the princess aloud. "I wonder how it is that some people are made to be so much happier than others! If I were that little girl, no one would ever call me naughty."

She gazed and gazed at the picture. At length she said to herself,

"I do not believe it is a picture. It is the real country, with a real hill, and a real little girl upon it. I shall soon see whether this isn't another of the old witch's cheats!"

She went close up to the picture, lifted her foot, and stepped over the frame.

"I am free, I am free!" she exclaimed; and she felt the wind upon her cheek.

The sound of a closing door struck on her ear. She turned—and there was a blank wall, without door or window, behind her. The hill with the sheep was before her, and she set out at once to reach it.

Now, if I am asked how this could be, I can only answer, that it was a result of the interaction of things outside and things inside, of the wise woman's skill, and the silly child's folly. If this does not satisfy my questioner, I can only add, that the wise woman was able to do far more wonderful things than this.

VI.

Meantime the wise woman was busy as she always was; and her business now was with the child of the shepherd and shepherdess, away in the north. Her name was Agnes.

Her father and mother were poor, and could not give her many things. Rosamond would have utterly despised the rude, simple playthings she had. Yet in one respect they were of more value far than hers: the king bought Rosamond's with his money; Agnes's father made hers with his hands.

And while Agnes had but few things—not seeing many things about her, and not even knowing that there were many things anywhere, she did not wish for many things, and was therefore neither covetous nor avaricious.

She played with the toys her father made her, and thought them the most wonderful things in the world—windmills, and little crooks, and water-wheels, and sometimes lambs made all of wool, and dolls made out of the leg-bones of sheep, which her mother dressed for her; and of such playthings she was never tired. Sometimes, however, she preferred playing with stones, which were plentiful, and flowers, which were few, or the brooks that ran down the hill, of which, although they were many, she could only play with one at a time, and that, indeed, troubled her a little—or live lambs that were not all wool, or the sheep-dogs, which were very friendly with her, and the best of playfellows, as she thought, for she had no human ones to compare them with. Neither was she greedy after nice things, but content, as well she might be, with the homely food provided for her. Nor was she by nature particularly self-willed or disobedient; she generally did what her father and mother wished, and believed what they told her. But by degrees they had spoiled her; and this was the way: they were so proud of her that they always repeated every thing she said, and told every thing she did, even when she was present; and so full of admiration of their child were they, that they wondered and laughed at and praised things in her which in another child would never have struck them as the least remarkable, and some things even which would in another have disgusted them altogether. Impertinent and rude things done by THEIR child they thought SO clever! laughing at them as something quite marvellous; her commonplace speeches were said over again as if they had been the finest poetry; and the pretty ways which every moderately good child has were extolled as if the result of her excellent taste, and the choice of her judgment and will. They would even say sometimes that she ought not to hear her own praises for fear it should make her vain, and then whisper them behind their hands, but so loud that she could not fail to hear every word. The consequence was that she soon came to believe—so soon, that she could not recall the time when she did not believe, as the most absolute fact in the universe, that she was SOMEBODY; that is, she became most immoderately conceited.

Now as the least atom of conceit is a thing to be ashamed of, you may fancy what she was like with such a quantity of it inside her!

At first it did not show itself outside in any very active form; but the wise woman had been to the cottage, and had seen her sitting alone, with such a smile of self-satisfaction upon her face as would have been quite startling to her, if she had ever been startled at any thing; for through that smile she could see lying at the root of it the worm that made it. For some smiles are like the ruddiness of certain apples, which is owing to a centipede, or other creeping thing, coiled up at the heart of them. Only her worm had a face and shape the very image of her own; and she looked so simpering, and mawkish, and self-conscious, and silly, that she made the wise woman feel rather sick.

Not that the child was a fool. Had she been, the wise woman would have only pitied and loved her, instead of feeling sick when she looked at her. She had very fair abilities, and were she once but made humble, would be capable not only of doing a good deal in time, but of beginning at once to grow to no end. But, if she were not made humble, her growing would be to a mass of distorted shapes all huddled together; so that, although the body she now showed might grow up straight and well-shaped and comely to behold, the new body that was growing inside of it, and would come out of it when she died, would be ugly, and crooked this way and that, like an aged hawthorn that has lived hundreds of years exposed upon all sides to salt sea-winds.

As time went on, this disease of self-conceit went on too, gradually devouring the good that was in her. For there is no fault that does not bring its brothers and sisters and cousins to live with it. By degrees, from thinking herself so clever, she came to fancy that whatever seemed to her, must of course be the correct judgment, and whatever she wished, the right thing; and grew so obstinate, that at length her parents feared to thwart her in any thing, knowing well that she would never give in. But there are victories far worse than defeats; and to overcome an angel too gentle to put out all his strength, and ride away in triumph on the back of a devil, is one of the poorest.

So long as she was left to take her own way and do as she would, she gave her parents little trouble. She would play about by herself in the little garden with its few hardy flowers, or amongst the heather where the bees were busy; or she would wander away amongst the hills, and be nobody knew where, sometimes from morning to night; nor did her parents venture to find fault with her.

She never went into rages like the princess, and would have thought Rosamond—oh, so ugly and vile! if she had seen her in one of her passions. But she was no better, for all that, and was quite as ugly in the eyes of the wise woman, who could not only see but read her face. What is there to choose between a face distorted to hideousness by anger, and one distorted to silliness by self-complacency? True, there is more hope of helping the angry child out of her form of selfishness than the conceited child out of hers; but on the other hand, the conceited child was not so terrible or dangerous as the wrathful one. The conceited one, however, was sometimes very angry, and then her anger was more spiteful than the other's; and, again, the wrathful one was often very conceited too. So that, on the whole, of two very unpleasant creatures, I would say that the king's daughter would have been the worse, had not the shepherd's been quite as bad. But, as I have said, the wise woman had her eye upon her: she saw that something special must be done, else she would be one of those who kneel to their own shadows till feet grow on their knees; then go down on their hands till their hands grow into feet; then lay their faces on the ground till they grow into snouts; when at last they are a hideous sort of lizards, each of which believes himself the best, wisest, and loveliest being in the world, yea, the very centre of the universe. And so they run about forever looking for their own shadows, that they may worship them, and miserable because they cannot find them, being themselves too near the ground to have any shadows; and what becomes of them at last there is but one who knows.

The wise woman, therefore, one day walked up to the door of the shepherd's cottage, dressed like a poor woman, and asked for a drink of water. The shepherd's wife looked at her, liked her, and brought her a cup of milk. The wise woman took it, for she made it a rule to accept every kindness that was offered her.

Agnes was not by nature a greedy girl, as I have said; but self-conceit will go far to generate every other vice under the sun. Vanity, which is a form of self-conceit, has repeatedly shown itself as the deepest feeling in the heart of a horrible murderess.

That morning, at breakfast, her mother had stinted her in milk—just a little—that she might have enough to make some milk-porridge for their dinner. Agnes did not mind it at the time, but when she saw the milk now given to a beggar, as she called the wise woman—though, surely, one might ask a draught of water, and accept a draught of milk, without being a beggar in any such sense as Agnes's contemptuous use of the word implied—a cloud came upon her forehead, and a double vertical wrinkle settled over her nose. The wise woman saw it, for all her business was with Agnes though she little knew it, and, rising, went and offered the cup to the child, where she sat with her knitting in a corner. Agnes looked at it, did not want it, was inclined to refuse it from a beggar, but thinking it would show her consequence to assert her rights, took it and drank it up. For whoever is possessed by a devil, judges with the mind of that devil; and hence Agnes was guilty of such a meanness as many who are themselves capable of something just as bad will consider incredible.

The wise woman waited till she had finished it—then, looking into the empty cup, said:

"You might have given me back as much as you had no claim upon!"

Agnes turned away and made no answer—far less from shame than indignation.

The wise woman looked at the mother.

"You should not have offered it to her if you did not mean her to have it," said the mother, siding with the devil in her child against the wise woman and her child too. Some foolish people think they take another's part when they take the part he takes.

The wise woman said nothing, but fixed her eyes upon her, and soon the mother hid her face in her apron weeping. Then she turned again to Agnes, who had never looked round but sat with her back to both, and suddenly lapped her in the folds of her cloak. When the mother again lifted her eyes, she had vanished.

Never supposing she had carried away her child, but uncomfortable because of what she had said to the poor woman, the mother went to the door, and called after her as she toiled slowly up the hill. But she never turned her head; and the mother went back into her cottage.

The wise woman walked close past the shepherd and his dogs, and through the midst of his flock of sheep. The shepherd wondered where she could be going—right up the hill. There was something strange about her too, he thought; and he followed her with his eyes as she went up and up.

It was near sunset, and as the sun went down, a gray cloud settled on the top of the mountain, which his last rays turned into a rosy gold. Straight into this cloud the shepherd saw the woman hold her pace, and in it she vanished. He little imagined that his child was under her cloak.

He went home as usual in the evening, but Agnes had not come in. They were accustomed to such an absence now and then, and were not at first frightened; but when it grew dark and she did not appear, the husband set out with his dogs in one direction, and the wife in another, to seek their child. Morning came and they had not found her. Then the whole countryside arose to search for the missing Agnes; but day after day and night after night passed, and nothing was discovered of or concerning her, until at length all gave up the search in despair except the mother, although she was nearly convinced now that the poor woman had carried her off.

One day she had wandered some distance from her cottage, thinking she might come upon the remains of her daughter at the foot of some cliff, when she came suddenly, instead, upon a disconsolate-looking creature sitting on a stone by the side of a stream.

Her hair hung in tangles from her head; her clothes were tattered, and through the rents her skin showed in many places; her cheeks were white, and worn thin with hunger; the hollows were dark under her eyes, and they stood out scared and wild. When she caught sight of the shepherdess, she jumped to her feet, and would have run away, but fell down in a faint.

At first sight the mother had taken her for her own child, but now she saw, with a pang of disappointment, that she had mistaken. Full of compassion, nevertheless, she said to herself:

"If she is not my Agnes, she is as much in need of help as if she were. If I cannot be good to my own, I will be as good as I can to some other woman's; and though I should scorn to be consoled for the loss of one by the presence of another, I yet may find some gladness in rescuing one child from the death which has taken the other."

Perhaps her words were not just like these, but her thoughts were. She took up the child, and carried her home. And this is how Rosamond came to occupy the place of the little girl whom she had envied in the picture.

VII.

Notwithstanding the differences between the two girls, which were, indeed, so many that most people would have said they were not in the least alike, they were the same in this, that each cared more for her own fancies and desires than for any thing else in the world. But I will tell you another difference: the princess was like several children in one—such was the variety of her moods; and in one mood she had no recollection or care about any thing whatever belonging to a previous mood—not even if it had left her but a moment before, and had been so violent as to make her ready to put her hand in the fire to get what she wanted. Plainly she was the mere puppet of her moods, and more than that, any cunning nurse who knew her well enough could call or send away those moods almost as she pleased, like a showman pulling strings behind a show. Agnes, on the contrary, seldom changed her mood, but kept that of calm assured self-satisfaction. Father nor mother had ever by wise punishment helped her to gain a victory over herself, and do what she did not like or choose; and their folly in reasoning with one unreasonable had fixed her in her conceit. She would actually nod her head to herself in complacent pride that she had stood out against them. This, however, was not so difficult as to justify even the pride of having conquered, seeing she loved them so little, and paid so little attention to the arguments and persuasions they used. Neither, when she found herself wrapped in the dark folds of the wise woman's cloak, did she behave in the least like the princess, for she was not afraid. "She'll soon set me down," she said, too self-important to suppose that any one would dare do her an injury.

Whether it be a good thing or a bad not to be afraid depends on what the fearlessness is founded upon. Some have no fear, because they have no knowledge of the danger: there is nothing fine in that. Some are too stupid to be afraid: there is nothing fine in that. Some who are not easily frightened would yet turn their backs and run, the moment they were frightened: such never had more courage than fear. But the man who will do his work in spite of his fear is a man of true courage. The fearlessness of Agnes was only ignorance: she did not know what it was to be hurt; she had never read a single story of giant, or ogress or wolf; and her mother had never carried out one of her threats of punishment. If the wise woman had but pinched her, she would have shown herself an abject little coward, trembling with fear at every change of motion so long as she carried her.

Nothing such, however, was in the wise woman's plan for the curing of her. On and on she carried her without a word. She knew that if she set her down she would never run after her like the princess, at least not before the evil thing was already upon her. On and on she went, never halting, never letting the light look in, or Agnes look out. She walked very fast, and got home to her cottage very soon after the princess had gone from it.

But she did not set Agnes down either in the cottage or in the great hall. She had other places, none of them alike. The place she had chosen for Agnes was a strange one—such a one as is to be found nowhere else in the wide world.

It was a great hollow sphere, made of a substance similar to that of the mirror which Rosamond had broken, but differently compounded. That substance no one could see by itself. It had neither door, nor window, nor any opening to break its perfect roundness.

The wise woman carried Agnes into a dark room, there undressed her, took from her hand her knitting-needles, and put her, naked as she was born, into the hollow sphere.

What sort of a place it was she could not tell. She could see nothing but a faint cold bluish light all about her. She could not feel that any thing supported her, and yet she did not sink. She stood for a while, perfectly calm, then sat down. Nothing bad could happen to HER—she was so important! And, indeed, it was but this: she had cared only for Somebody, and now she was going to have only Somebody. Her own choice was going to be carried a good deal farther for her than she would have knowingly carried it for herself.

After sitting a while, she wished she had something to do, but nothing came. A little longer, and it grew wearisome. She would see whether she could not walk out of the strange luminous dusk that surrounded her.

Walk she found she could, well enough, but walk out she could not. On and on she went, keeping as much in a straight line as she might, but after walking until she was thoroughly tired, she found herself no nearer out of her prison than before. She had not, indeed, advanced a single step; for, in whatever direction she tried to go, the sphere turned round and round, answering her feet accordingly. Like a squirrel in his cage she but kept placing another spot of the cunningly suspended sphere under her feet, and she would have been still only at its lowest point after walking for ages.

At length she cried aloud; but there was no answer. It grew dreary and drearier—in her, that is: outside there was no change. Nothing was overhead, nothing under foot, nothing on either hand, but the same pale, faint, bluish glimmer. She wept at last, then grew very angry, and then sullen; but nobody heeded whether she cried or laughed. It was all the same to the cold unmoving twilight that rounded her. On and on went the dreary hours—or did they go at all?—"no change, no pause, no hope;"—on and on till she FELT she was forgotten, and then she grew strangely still and fell asleep.

The moment she was asleep, the wise woman came, lifted her out, and laid her in her bosom; fed her with a wonderful milk, which she received without knowing it; nursed her all the night long, and, just ere she woke, laid her back in the blue sphere again.

When first she came to herself, she thought the horrors of the preceding day had been all a dream of the night. But they soon asserted themselves as facts, for here they were!—nothing to see but a cold blue light, and nothing to do but see it. Oh, how slowly the hours went by! She lost all notion of time. If she had been told that she had been there twenty years, she would have believed it—or twenty minutes—it would have been all the same: except for weariness, time was for her no more.

Another night came, and another still, during both of which the wise woman nursed and fed her. But she knew nothing of that, and the same one dreary day seemed ever brooding over her.

All at once, on the third day, she was aware that a naked child was seated beside her. But there was something about the child that made her shudder. She never looked at Agnes, but sat with her chin sunk on her chest, and her eyes staring at her own toes. She was the color of pale earth, with a pinched nose, and a mere slit in her face for a mouth.

"How ugly she is!" thought Agnes. "What business has she beside me!"

But it was so lonely that she would have been glad to play with a serpent, and put out her hand to touch her. She touched nothing. The child, also, put out her hand—but in the direction away from Agnes. And that was well, for if she had touched Agnes it would have killed her. Then Agnes said, "Who are you?" And the little girl said, "Who are you?" "I am Agnes," said Agnes; and the little girl said, "I am Agnes." Then Agnes thought she was mocking her, and said, "You are ugly;" and the little girl said, "You are ugly."

Then Agnes lost her temper, and put out her hands to seize the little girl; but lo! the little girl was gone, and she found herself tugging at her own hair. She let go; and there was the little girl again! Agnes was furious now, and flew at her to bite her. But she found her teeth in her own arm, and the little girl was gone—only to return again; and each time she came back she was tenfold uglier than before. And now Agnes hated her with her whole heart.

The moment she hated her, it flashed upon her with a sickening disgust that the child was not another, but her Self, her Somebody, and that she was now shut up with her for ever and ever—no more for one moment ever to be alone. In her agony of despair, sleep descended, and she slept.

When she woke, there was the little girl, heedless, ugly, miserable, staring at her own toes. All at once, the creature began to smile, but with such an odious, self-satisfied expression, that Agnes felt ashamed of seeing her. Then she began to pat her own cheeks, to stroke her own body, and examine her finger-ends, nodding her head with satisfaction. Agnes felt that there could not be such another hateful, ape-like creature, and at the same time was perfectly aware she was only doing outside of her what she herself had been doing, as long as she could remember, inside of her.

She turned sick at herself, and would gladly have been put out of existence, but for three days the odious companionship went on. By the third day, Agnes was not merely sick but ashamed of the life she had hitherto led, was despicable in her own eyes, and astonished that she had never seen the truth concerning herself before.

The next morning she woke in the arms of the wise woman; the horror had vanished from her sight, and two heavenly eyes were gazing upon her. She wept and clung to her, and the more she clung, the more tenderly did the great strong arms close around her.

When she had lain thus for a while, the wise woman carried her into her cottage, and washed her in the little well; then dressed her in clean garments, and gave her bread and milk. When she had eaten it, she called her to her, and said very solemnly,—

"Agnes, you must not imagine you are cured. That you are ashamed of yourself now is no sign that the cause for such shame has ceased. In new circumstances, especially after you have done well for a while, you will be in danger of thinking just as much of yourself as before. So beware of yourself. I am going from home, and leave you in charge of the house. Do just as I tell you till my return."

She then gave her the same directions she had formerly given Rosamond—with this difference, that she told her to go into the picture-hall when she pleased, showing her the entrance, against which the clock no longer stood—and went away, closing the door behind her.

VIII.

As soon as she was left alone, Agnes set to work tidying and dusting the cottage, made up the fire, watered the bed, and cleaned the inside of the windows: the wise woman herself always kept the outside of them clean. When she had done, she found her dinner—of the same sort she was used to at home, but better—in the hole of the wall. When she had eaten it, she went to look at the pictures.

By this time her old disposition had begun to rouse again. She had been doing her duty, and had in consequence begun again to think herself Somebody. However strange it may well seem, to do one's duty will make any one conceited who only does it sometimes. Those who do it always would as soon think of being conceited of eating their dinner as of doing their duty. What honest boy would pride himself on not picking pockets? A thief who was trying to reform would. To be conceited of doing one's duty is then a sign of how little one does it, and how little one sees what a contemptible thing it is not to do it. Could any but a low creature be conceited of not being contemptible? Until our duty becomes to us common as breathing, we are poor creatures.

So Agnes began to stroke herself once more, forgetting her late self-stroking companion, and never reflecting that she was now doing what she had then abhorred. And in this mood she went into the picture-gallery.

The first picture she saw represented a square in a great city, one side of which was occupied by a splendid marble palace, with great flights of broad steps leading up to the door. Between it and the square was a marble-paved court, with gates of brass, at which stood sentries in gorgeous uniforms, and to which was affixed the following proclamation in letters of gold, large enough for Agnes to read:—

"By the will of the King, from this time until further notice, every stray child found in the realm shall be brought without a moment's delay to the palace. Whoever shall be found having done otherwise shall straightway lose his head by the hand of the public executioner."

Agnes's heart beat loud, and her face flushed.

"Can there be such a city in the world?" she said to herself. "If I only knew where it was, I should set out for it at once. THERE would be the place for a clever girl like me!"

Her eyes fell on the picture which had so enticed Rosamond. It was the very country where her father fed his flocks. Just round the shoulder of the hill was the cottage where her parents lived, where she was born and whence she had been carried by the beggar-woman.

"Ah!" she said, "they didn't know me there. They little thought what I could be, if I had the chance. If I were but in this good, kind, loving, generous king's palace, I should soon be such a great lady as they never saw! Then they would understand what a good little girl I had always been! And I shouldn't forget my poor parents like some I have read of. I would be generous. I should never be selfish and proud like girls in story-books!"

As she said this, she turned her back with disdain upon the picture of her home, and setting herself before the picture of the palace, stared at it with wide ambitious eyes, and a heart whose every beat was a throb of arrogant self-esteem.

The shepherd-child was now worse than ever the poor princess had been. For the wise woman had given her a terrible lesson one of which the princess was not capable, and she had known what it meant; yet here she was as bad as ever, therefore worse than before. The ugly creature whose presence had made her so miserable had indeed crept out of sight and mind too—but where was she? Nestling in her very heart, where most of all she had her company, and least of all could see her. The wise woman had called her out, that Agnes might see what sort of creature she was herself; but now she was snug in her soul's bed again, and she did not even suspect she was there.

After gazing a while at the palace picture, during which her ambitious pride rose and rose, she turned yet again in condescending mood, and honored the home picture with one stare more.

"What a poor, miserable spot it is compared with this lordly palace!" she said.

But presently she spied something in it she had not seen before, and drew nearer. It was the form of a little girl, building a bridge of stones over one of the hill-brooks.

"Ah, there I am myself!" she said. "That is just how I used to do.—No," she resumed, "it is not me. That snub-nosed little fright could never be meant for me! It was the frock that made me think so. But it IS a picture of the place. I declare, I can see the smoke of the cottage rising from behind the hill! What a dull, dirty, insignificant spot it is! And what a life to lead there!"

She turned once more to the city picture. And now a strange thing took place. In proportion as the other, to the eyes of her mind, receded into the background, this, to her present bodily eyes, appeared to come forward and assume reality. At last, after it had been in this way growing upon her for some time, she gave a cry of conviction, and said aloud,—

"I do believe it is real! That frame is only a trick of the woman to make me fancy it a picture lest I should go and make my fortune. She is a witch, the ugly old creature! It would serve her right to tell the king and have her punished for not taking me to the palace—one of his poor lost children he is so fond of! I should like to see her ugly old head cut off. Anyhow I will try my luck without asking her leave. How she has ill used me!"

But at that moment, she heard the voice of the wise woman calling, "Agnes!" and, smoothing her face, she tried to look as good as she could, and walked back into the cottage. There stood the wise woman, looking all round the place, and examining her work. She fixed her eyes upon Agnes in a way that confused her, and made her cast hers down, for she felt as if she were reading her thoughts. The wise woman, however, asked no questions, but began to talk about her work, approving of some of it, which filled her with arrogance, and showing how some of it might have been done better, which filled her with resentment. But the wise woman seemed to take no care of what she might be thinking, and went straight on with her lesson. By the time it was over, the power of reading thoughts would not have been necessary to a knowledge of what was in the mind of Agnes, for it had all come to the surface—that is up into her face, which is the surface of the mind. Ere it had time to sink down again, the wise woman caught up the little mirror, and held it before her: Agnes saw her Somebody—the very embodiment of miserable conceit and ugly ill-temper. She gave such a scream of horror that the wise woman pitied her, and laying aside the mirror, took her upon her knees, and talked to her most kindly and solemnly; in particular about the necessity of destroying the ugly things that come out of the heart—so ugly that they make the very face over them ugly also.

And what was Agnes doing all the time the wise woman was talking to her? Would you believe it?—instead of thinking how to kill the ugly things in her heart, she was with all her might resolving to be more careful of her face, that is, to keep down the things in her heart so that they should not show in her face, she was resolving to be a hypocrite as well as a self-worshipper. Her heart was wormy, and the worms were eating very fast at it now.

Then the wise woman laid her gently down upon the heather-bed, and she fell fast asleep, and had an awful dream about her Somebody.

When she woke in the morning, instead of getting up to do the work of the house, she lay thinking—to evil purpose. In place of taking her dream as a warning, and thinking over what the wise woman had said the night before, she communed with herself in this fashion:—

"If I stay here longer, I shall be miserable, It is nothing better than slavery. The old witch shows me horrible things in the day to set me dreaming horrible things in the night. If I don't run away, that frightful blue prison and the disgusting girl will come back, and I shall go out of my mind. How I do wish I could find the way to the good king's palace! I shall go and look at the picture again—if it be a picture—as soon as I've got my clothes on. The work can wait. It's not my work. It's the old witch's; and she ought to do it herself."

She jumped out of bed, and hurried on her clothes. There was no wise woman to be seen; and she hastened into the hall. There was the picture, with the marble palace, and the proclamation shining in letters of gold upon its gates of brass. She stood before it, and gazed and gazed; and all the time it kept growing upon her in some strange way, until at last she was fully persuaded that it was no picture, but a real city, square, and marble palace, seen through a framed opening in the wall. She ran up to the frame, stepped over it, felt the wind blow upon her cheek, heard the sound of a closing door behind her, and was free. FREE was she, with that creature inside her?

The same moment a terrible storm of thunder and lightning, wind and rain, came on. The uproar was appalling. Agnes threw herself upon the ground, hid her face in her hands, and there lay until it was over. As soon as she felt the sun shining on her, she rose. There was the city far away on the horizon. Without once turning to take a farewell look of the place she was leaving, she set off, as fast as her feet would carry her, in the direction of the city. So eager was she, that again and again she fell, but only to get up, and run on faster than before.

IX.

The shepherdess carried Rosamond home, gave her a warm bath in the tub in which she washed her linen, made her some bread-and-milk, and after she had eaten it, put her to bed in Agnes's crib, where she slept all the rest of that day and all the following night.

When at last she opened her eyes, it was to see around her a far poorer cottage than the one she had left—very bare and uncomfortable indeed, she might well have thought; but she had come through such troubles of late, in the way of hunger and weariness and cold and fear, that she was not altogether in her ordinary mood of fault-finding, and so was able to lie enjoying the thought that at length she was safe, and going to be fed and kept warm. The idea of doing any thing in return for shelter and food and clothes, did not, however, even cross her mind.

But the shepherdess was one of that plentiful number who can be wiser concerning other women's children than concerning their own. Such will often give you very tolerable hints as to how you ought to manage your children, and will find fault neatly enough with the system you are trying to carry out; but all their wisdom goes off in talking, and there is none left for doing what they have themselves said. There is one road talk never finds, and that is the way into the talker's own hands and feet. And such never seem to know themselves—not even when they are reading about themselves in print. Still, not being specially blinded in any direction but their own, they can sometimes even act with a little sense towards children who are not theirs. They are affected with a sort of blindness like that which renders some people incapable of seeing, except sideways.

She came up to the bed, looked at the princess, and saw that she was better. But she did not like her much. There was no mark of a princess about her, and never had been since she began to run alone. True, hunger had brought down her fat cheeks, but it had not turned down her impudent nose, or driven the sullenness and greed from her mouth. Nothing but the wise woman could do that—and not even she, without the aid of the princess herself. So the shepherdess thought what a poor substitute she had got for her own lovely Agnes—who was in fact equally repulsive, only in a way to which she had got used; for the selfishness in her love had blinded her to the thin pinched nose and the mean self-satisfied mouth. It was well for the princess, though, sad as it is to say, that the shepherdess did not take to her, for then she would most likely have only done her harm instead of good.

"Now, my girl," she said, "you must get up, and do something. We can't keep idle folk here."

"I'm not a folk," said Rosamond; "I'm a princess."

"A pretty princess—with a nose like that! And all in rags too! If you tell such stories, I shall soon let you know what I think of you."

Rosamond then understood that the mere calling herself a princess, without having any thing to show for it, was of no use. She obeyed and rose, for she was hungry; but she had to sweep the floor ere she had any thing to eat.

The shepherd came in to breakfast, and was kinder than his wife. He took her up in his arms and would have kissed her; but she took it as an insult from a man whose hands smelt of tar, and kicked and screamed with rage. The poor man, finding he had made a mistake, set her down at once. But to look at the two, one might well have judged it condescension rather than rudeness in such a man to kiss such a child. He was tall, and almost stately, with a thoughtful forehead, bright eyes, eagle nose, and gentle mouth; while the princess was such as I have described her.

Not content with being set down and let alone, she continued to storm and scold at the shepherd, crying she was a princess, and would like to know what right he had to touch her! But he only looked down upon her from the height of his tall person with a benignant smile, regarding her as a spoiled little ape whose mother had flattered her by calling her a princess.

"Turn her out of doors, the ungrateful hussy!" cried his wife. "With your bread and your milk inside her ugly body, this is what she gives you for it! Troth, I'm paid for carrying home such an ill-bred tramp in my arms! My own poor angel Agnes! As if that ill-tempered toad were one hair like her!"

These words drove the princess beside herself; for those who are most given to abuse can least endure it. With fists and feet and teeth, as was her wont, she rushed at the shepherdess, whose hand was already raised to deal her a sound box on the ear, when a better appointed minister of vengeance suddenly showed himself. Bounding in at the cottage-door came one of the sheep-dogs, who was called Prince, and whom I shall not refer to with a WHICH, because he was a very superior animal indeed, even for a sheep-dog, which is the most intelligent of dogs: he flew at the princess, knocked her down, and commenced shaking her so violently as to tear her miserable clothes to pieces. Used, however, to mouthing little lambs, he took care not to hurt her much, though for her good he left her a blue nip or two by way of letting her imagine what biting might be. His master, knowing he would not injure her, thought it better not to call him off, and in half a minute he left her of his own accord, and, casting a glance of indignant rebuke behind him as he went, walked slowly to the hearth, where he laid himself down with his tail toward her. She rose, terrified almost to death, and would have crept again into Agnes's crib for refuge; but the shepherdess cried—

"Come, come, princess! I'll have no skulking to bed in the good daylight. Go and clean your master's Sunday boots there."

"I will not!" screamed the princess, and ran from the house.

"Prince!" cried the shepherdess, and up jumped the dog, and looked in her face, wagging his bushy tail.

"Fetch her back," she said, pointing to the door.

With two or three bounds Prince caught the princess, again threw her down, and taking her by her clothes dragged her back into the cottage, and dropped her at his mistress' feet, where she lay like a bundle of rags.

"Get up," said the shepherdess.

Rosamond got up as pale as death.

"Go and clean the boots."

"I don't know how."

"Go and try. There are the brushes, and yonder is the blacking-pot."

Instructing her how to black boots, it came into the thought of the shepherdess what a fine thing it would be if she could teach this miserable little wretch, so forsaken and ill-bred, to be a good, well-behaved, respectable child. She was hardly the woman to do it, but every thing well meant is a help, and she had the wisdom to beg her husband to place Prince under her orders for a while, and not take him to the hill as usual, that he might help her in getting the princess into order.

When the husband was gone, and his boots, with the aid of her own finishing touches, at last quite respectably brushed, the shepherdess told the princess that she might go and play for a while, only she must not go out of sight of the cottage-door.

The princess went right gladly, with the firm intention, however, of getting out of sight by slow degrees, and then at once taking to her heels. But no sooner was she over the threshold than the shepherdess said to the dog, "Watch her;" and out shot Prince.

The moment she saw him, Rosamond threw herself on her face, trembling from head to foot. But the dog had no quarrel with her, and of the violence against which he always felt bound to protest in dog fashion, there was no sign in the prostrate shape before him; so he poked his nose under her, turned her over, and began licking her face and hands. When she saw that he meant to be friendly, her love for animals, which had had no indulgence for a long time now, came wide awake, and in a little while they were romping and rushing about, the best friends in the world.

Having thus seen one enemy, as she thought, changed to a friend, she began to resume her former plan, and crept cunningly farther and farther. At length she came to a little hollow, and instantly rolled down into it. Finding then that she was out of sight of the cottage, she ran off at full speed.

But she had not gone more than a dozen paces, when she heard a growling rush behind her, and the next instant was on the ground, with the dog standing over her, showing his teeth, and flaming at her with his eyes. She threw her arms round his neck, and immediately he licked her face, and let her get up. But the moment she would have moved a step farther from the cottage, there he was it front of her, growling, and showing his teeth. She saw it was of no use, and went back with him.

Thus was the princess provided with a dog for a private tutor—just the right sort for her.

Presently the shepherdess appeared at the door and called her. She would have disregarded the summons, but Prince did his best to let her know that, until she could obey herself, she must obey him. So she went into the cottage, and there the shepherdess ordered her to peel the potatoes for dinner. She sulked and refused. Here Prince could do nothing to help his mistress, but she had not to go far to find another ally.

"Very well, Miss Princess!" she said; "we shall soon see how you like to go without when dinner-time comes."

Now the princess had very little foresight, and the idea of future hunger would have moved her little; but happily, from her game of romps with Prince, she had begun to be hungry already, and so the threat had force. She took the knife and began to peel the potatoes.

By slow degrees the princess improved a little. A few more outbreaks of passion, and a few more savage attacks from Prince, and she had learned to try to restrain herself when she felt the passion coming on; while a few dinnerless afternoons entirely opened her eyes to the necessity of working in order to eat. Prince was her first, and Hunger her second dog-counsellor.

But a still better thing was that she soon grew very fond of Prince. Towards the gaining of her affections, he had three advantages: first, his nature was inferior to hers; next, he was a beast; and last, she was afraid of him; for so spoiled was she that she could more easily love what was below than what was above her, and a beast, than one of her own kind, and indeed could hardly have ever come to love any thing much that she had not first learned to fear, and the white teeth and flaming eyes of the angry Prince were more terrible to her than any thing had yet been, except those of the wolf, which she had now forgotten. Then again, he was such a delightful playfellow, that so long as she neither lost her temper, nor went against orders, she might do almost any thing she pleased with him. In fact, such was his influence upon her, that she who had scoffed at the wisest woman in the whole world, and derided the wishes of her own father and mother, came at length to regard this dog as a superior being, and to look up to him as well as love him. And this was best of all.

The improvement upon her, in the course of a month, was plain. She had quite ceased to go into passions, and had actually begun to take a little interest in her work and try to do it well.

Still, the change was mostly an outside one. I do not mean that she was pretending. Indeed she had never been given to pretence of any sort. But the change was not in HER, only in her mood. A second change of circumstances would have soon brought a second change of behavior; and, so long as that was possible, she continued the same sort of person she had always been. But if she had not gained much, a trifle had been gained for her: a little quietness and order of mind, and hence a somewhat greater possibility of the first idea of right arising in it, whereupon she would begin to see what a wretched creature she was, and must continue until she herself was right.

Meantime the wise woman had been watching her when she least fancied it, and taking note of the change that was passing upon her. Out of the large eyes of a gentle sheep she had been watching her—a sheep that puzzled the shepherd; for every now and then she would appear in his flock, and he would catch sight of her two or three times in a day, sometimes for days together, yet he never saw her when he looked for her, and never when he counted the flock into the fold at night. He knew she was not one of his; but where could she come from, and where could she go to? For there was no other flock within many miles, and he never could get near enough to her to see whether or not she was marked. Nor was Prince of the least use to him for the unravelling of the mystery; for although, as often as he told him to fetch the strange sheep, he went bounding to her at once, it was only to lie down at her feet.

At length, however, the wise woman had made up her mind, and after that the strange sheep no longer troubled the shepherd.

As Rosamond improved, the shepherdess grew kinder. She gave her all Agnes's clothes, and began to treat her much more like a daughter. Hence she had a great deal of liberty after the little work required of her was over, and would often spend hours at a time with the shepherd, watching the sheep and the dogs, and learning a little from seeing how Prince, and the others as well, managed their charge—how they never touched the sheep that did as they were told and turned when they were bid, but jumped on a disobedient flock, and ran along their backs, biting, and barking, and half choking themselves with mouthfuls of their wool.

Then also she would play with the brooks, and learn their songs, and build bridges over them. And sometimes she would be seized with such delight of heart that she would spread out her arms to the wind, and go rushing up the hill till her breath left her, when she would tumble down in the heather, and lie there till it came back again.

A noticeable change had by this time passed also on her countenance. Her coarse shapeless mouth had begun to show a glimmer of lines and curves about it, and the fat had not returned with the roses to her cheeks, so that her eyes looked larger than before; while, more noteworthy still, the bridge of her nose had grown higher, so that it was less of the impudent, insignificant thing inherited from a certain great-great-great-grandmother, who had little else to leave her. For a long time, it had fitted her very well, for it was just like her; but now there was ground for alteration, and already the granny who gave it her would not have recognized it. It was growing a little liker Prince's; and Prince's was a long, perceptive, sagacious nose,—one that was seldom mistaken.

One day about noon, while the sheep were mostly lying down, and the shepherd, having left them to the care of the dogs, was himself stretched under the shade of a rock a little way apart, and the princess sat knitting, with Prince at her feet, lying in wait for a snap at a great fly, for even he had his follies—Rosamond saw a poor woman come toiling up the hill, but took little notice of her until she was passing, a few yards off, when she heard her utter the dog's name in a low voice.

Immediately on the summons, Prince started up and followed her—with hanging head, but gently-wagging tail. At first the princess thought he was merely taking observations, and consulting with his nose whether she was respectable or not, but she soon saw that he was following her in meek submission. Then she sprung to her feet and cried, "Prince, Prince!" But Prince only turned his head and gave her an odd look, as if he were trying to smile, and could not. Then the princess grew angry, and ran after him, shouting, "Prince, come here directly." Again Prince turned his head, but this time to growl and show his teeth.

The princess flew into one of her forgotten rages, and picking up a stone, flung it at the woman. Prince turned and darted at her, with fury in his eyes, and his white teeth gleaming. At the awful sight the princess turned also, and would have fled, but he was upon her in a moment, and threw her to the ground, and there she lay.

It was evening when she came to herself. A cool twilight wind, that somehow seemed to come all the way from the stars, was blowing upon her. The poor woman and Prince, the shepherd and his sheep, were all gone, and she was left alone with the wind upon the heather.

She felt sad, weak, and, perhaps, for the first time in her life, a little ashamed. The violence of which she had been guilty had vanished from her spirit, and now lay in her memory with the calm morning behind it, while in front the quiet dusky night was now closing in the loud shame betwixt a double peace. Between the two her passion looked ugly. It pained her to remember. She felt it was hateful, and HERS.

But, alas, Prince was gone! That horrid woman had taken him away! The fury rose again in her heart, and raged—until it came to her mind how her dear Prince would have flown at her throat if he had seen her in such a passion. The memory calmed her, and she rose and went home. There, perhaps, she would find Prince, for surely he could never have been such a silly dog as go away altogether with a strange woman!

She opened the door and went in. Dogs were asleep all about the cottage, it seemed to her, but nowhere was Prince. She crept away to her little bed, and cried herself asleep.

In the morning the shepherd and shepherdess were indeed glad to find she had come home, for they thought she had run away.

"Where is Prince?" she cried, the moment she waked.

"His mistress has taken him," answered the shepherd.

"Was that woman his mistress?"

"I fancy so. He followed her as if he had known her all his life. I am very sorry to lose him, though."

The poor woman had gone close past the rock where the shepherd lay. He saw her coming, and thought of the strange sheep which had been feeding beside him when he lay down. "Who can she be?" he said to himself; but when he noted how Prince followed her, without even looking up at him as he passed, he remembered how Prince had come to him. And this was how: as he lay in bed one fierce winter morning, just about to rise, he heard the voice of a woman call to him through the storm, "Shepherd, I have brought you a dog. Be good to him. I will come again and fetch him away." He dressed as quickly as he could, and went to the door. It was half snowed up, but on the top of the white mound before it stood Prince. And now he had gone as mysteriously as he had come, and he felt sad.

Rosamond was very sorry too, and hence when she saw the looks of the shepherd and shepherdess, she was able to understand them. And she tried for a while to behave better to them because of their sorrow. So the loss of the dog brought them all nearer to each other.

X.

After the thunder-storm, Agnes did not meet with a single obstruction or misadventure. Everybody was strangely polite, gave her whatever she desired, and answered her questions, but asked none in return, and looked all the time as if her departure would be a relief. They were afraid, in fact, from her appearance, lest she should tell them that she was lost, when they would be bound, on pain of public execution, to take her to the palace.

But no sooner had she entered the city than she saw it would hardly do to present herself as a lost child at the palace-gates; for how were they to know that she was not an impostor, especially since she really was one, having run away from the wise woman? So she wandered about looking at every thing until she was tired, and bewildered by the noise and confusion all around her. The wearier she got, the more was she pushed in every direction. Having been used to a whole hill to wander upon, she was very awkward in the crowded streets, and often on the point of being run over by the horses, which seemed to her to be going every way like a frightened flock. She spoke to several persons, but no one stopped to answer her; and at length, her courage giving way, she felt lost indeed, and began to cry. A soldier saw her, and asked what was the matter.

"I've nowhere to go to," she sobbed.

"Where's your mother?" asked the soldier.

"I don't know," answered Agnes. "I was carried off by an old woman, who then went away and left me. I don't know where she is, or where I am myself."

"Come," said the soldier, "this is a case for his Majesty."

So saying, he took her by the hand, led her to the palace, and begged an audience of the king and queen. The porter glanced at Agnes, immediately admitted them, and showed them into a great splendid room, where the king and queen sat every day to review lost children, in the hope of one day thus finding their Rosamond. But they were by this time beginning to get tired of it. The moment they cast their eyes upon Agnes, the queen threw back her head, threw up her hands, and cried, "What a miserable, conceited, white-faced little ape!" and the king turned upon the soldier in wrath, and cried, forgetting his own decree, "What do you mean by bringing such a dirty, vulgar-looking, pert creature into my palace? The dullest soldier in my army could never for a moment imagine a child like THAT, one hair's-breadth like the lovely angel we lost!"

"I humbly beg your Majesty's pardon," said the soldier, "but what was I to do? There stands your Majesty's proclamation in gold letters on the brazen gates of the palace."

"I shall have it taken down," said the king. "Remove the child."

"Please your Majesty, what am I to do with her?"

"Take her home with you."

"I have six already, sire, and do not want her."

"Then drop her where you picked her up."

"If I do, sire, some one else will find her and bring her back to your Majesties."

"That will never do," said the king. "I cannot bear to look at her."

"For all her ugliness," said the queen, "she is plainly lost, and so is our Rosamond."

"It may be only a pretence, to get into the palace," said the king.

"Take her to the head scullion, soldier," said the queen, "and tell her to make her useful. If she should find out she has been pretending to be lost, she must let me know."

The soldier was so anxious to get rid of her, that he caught her up in his arms, hurried her from the room, found his way to the scullery, and gave her, trembling with fear, in charge to the head maid, with the queen's message.

As it was evident that the queen had no favor for her, the servants did as they pleased with her, and often treated her harshly. Not one amongst them liked her, nor was it any wonder, seeing that, with every step she took from the wise woman's house, she had grown more contemptible, for she had grown more conceited. Every civil answer given her, she attributed to the impression she made, not to the desire to get rid of her; and every kindness, to approbation of her looks and speech, instead of friendliness to a lonely child. Hence by this time she was twice as odious as before; for whoever has had such severe treatment as the wise woman gave her, and is not the better for it, always grows worse than before. They drove her about, boxed her ears on the smallest provocation, laid every thing to her charge, called her all manner of contemptuous names, jeered and scoffed at her awkwardnesses, and made her life so miserable that she was in a fair way to forget every thing she had learned, and know nothing but how to clean saucepans and kettles.

They would not have been so hard upon her, however, but for her irritating behavior. She dared not refuse to do as she was told, but she obeyed now with a pursed-up mouth, and now with a contemptuous smile. The only thing that sustained her was her constant contriving how to get out of the painful position in which she found herself. There is but one true way, however, of getting out of any position we may be in, and that is, to do the work of it so well that we grow fit for a better: I need not say this was not the plan upon which Agnes was cunning enough to fix.

She had soon learned from the talk around her the reason of the proclamation which had brought her hither.

"Was the lost princess so very beautiful?" she said one day to the youngest of her fellow-servants.

"Beautiful!" screamed the maid; "she was just the ugliest little toad you ever set eyes upon."

"What was she like?" asked Agnes.

"She was about your size, and quite as ugly, only not in the same way; for she had red cheeks, and a cocked little nose, and the biggest, ugliest mouth you ever saw."

Agnes fell a-thinking.

"Is there a picture of her anywhere in the palace?" she asked.

"How should I know? You can ask a housemaid."

Agnes soon learned that there was one, and contrived to get a peep of it. Then she was certain of what she had suspected from the description given of her, namely, that she was the same she had seen in the picture at the wise woman's house. The conclusion followed, that the lost princess must be staying with her father and mother, for assuredly in the picture she wore one of her frocks.

She went to the head scullion, and with humble manner, but proud heart, begged her to procure for her the favor of a word with the queen.

"A likely thing indeed!" was the answer, accompanied by a resounding box on the ear.

She tried the head cook next, but with no better success, and so was driven to her meditations again, the result of which was that she began to drop hints that she knew something about the princess. This came at length to the queen's ears, and she sent for her.

Absorbed in her own selfish ambitions, Agnes never thought of the risk to which she was about to expose her parents, but told the queen that in her wanderings she had caught sight of just such a lovely creature as she described the princess, only dressed like a peasant—saying, that, if the king would permit her to go and look for her, she had little doubt of bringing her back safe and sound within a few weeks.

But although she spoke the truth, she had such a look of cunning on her pinched face, that the queen could not possibly trust her, but believed that she made the proposal merely to get away, and have money given her for her journey. Still there was a chance, and she would not say any thing until she had consulted the king.

Then they had Agnes up before the lord chancellor, who, after much questioning of her, arrived at last, he thought, at some notion of the part of the country described by her—that was, if she spoke the truth, which, from her looks and behavior, he also considered entirely doubtful. Thereupon she was ordered back to the kitchen, and a band of soldiers, under a clever lawyer, sent out to search every foot of the supposed region. They were commanded not to return until they brought with them, bound hand and foot, such a shepherd pair as that of which they received a full description.

And now Agnes was worse off than before. For to her other miseries was added the fear of what would befall her when it was discovered that the persons of whom they were in quest, and whom she was certain they must find, were her own father and mother.

By this time the king and queen were so tired of seeing lost children, genuine or pretended—for they cared for no child any longer than there seemed a chance of its turning out their child—that with this new hope, which, however poor and vague at first, soon began to grow upon such imaginations as they had, they commanded the proclamation to be taken down from the palace gates, and directed the various sentries to admit no child whatever, lost or found, be the reason or pretence what it might, until further orders.

"I'm sick of children!" said the king to his secretary, as he finished dictating the direction.

XI.

After Prince was gone, the princess, by degrees, fell back into some of her bad old ways, from which only the presence of the dog, not her own betterment, had kept her. She never grew nearly so selfish again, but she began to let her angry old self lift up its head once more, until by and by she grew so bad that the shepherdess declared she should not stop in the house a day longer, for she was quite unendurable.

"It is all very well for you, husband," she said, "for you haven't her all day about you, and only see the best of her. But if you had her in work instead of play hours, you would like her no better than I do. And then it's not her ugly passions only, but when she's in one of her tantrums, it's impossible to get any work out of her. At such times she's just as obstinate as—as—as"—

She was going to say "as Agnes," but the feelings of a mother overcame her, and she could not utter the words.

"In fact," she said instead, "she makes my life miserable."

The shepherd felt he had no right to tell his wife she must submit to have her life made miserable, and therefore, although he was really much attached to Rosamond, he would not interfere; and the shepherdess told her she must look out for another place.

The princess was, however, this much better than before, even in respect of her passions, that they were not quite so bad, and after one was over, she was really ashamed of it. But not once, ever since the departure of Prince had she tried to check the rush of the evil temper when it came upon her. She hated it when she was out of it, and that was something; but while she was in it, she went full swing with it wherever the prince of the power of it pleased to carry her. Nor was this all: although she might by this time have known well enough that as soon as she was out of it she was certain to be ashamed of it, she would yet justify it to herself with twenty different arguments that looked very good at the time, but would have looked very poor indeed afterwards, if then she had ever remembered them.

She was not sorry to leave the shepherd's cottage, for she felt certain of soon finding her way back to her father and mother; and she would, indeed, have set out long before, but that her foot had somehow got hurt when Prince gave her his last admonition, and she had never since been able for long walks, which she sometimes blamed as the cause of her temper growing worse. But if people are good-tempered only when they are comfortable, what thanks have they?—Her foot was now much better; and as soon as the shepherdess had thus spoken, she resolved to set out at once, and work or beg her way home. At the moment she was quite unmindful of what she owed the good people, and, indeed, was as yet incapable of understanding a tenth part of her obligation to them. So she bade them good by without a tear, and limped her way down the hill, leaving the shepherdess weeping, and the shepherd looking very grave.

When she reached the valley she followed the course of the stream, knowing only that it would lead her away from the hill where the sheep fed, into richer lands where were farms and cattle. Rounding one of the roots of the hill she saw before her a poor woman walking slowly along the road with a burden of heather upon her back, and presently passed her, but had gone only a few paces farther when she heard her calling after her in a kind old voice—

"Your shoe-tie is loose, my child."

But Rosamond was growing tired, for her foot had become painful, and so she was cross, and neither returned answer, nor paid heed to the warning. For when we are cross, all our other faults grow busy, and poke up their ugly heads like maggots, and the princess's old dislike to doing any thing that came to her with the least air of advice about it returned in full force.

"My child," said the woman again, "if you don't fasten your shoe-tie, it will make you fall."

"Mind your own business," said Rosamond, without even turning her head, and had not gone more than three steps when she fell flat on her face on the path. She tried to get up, but the effort forced from her a scream, for she had sprained the ankle of the foot that was already lame.

The old woman was by her side instantly.

"Where are you hurt, child?" she asked, throwing down her burden and kneeling beside her.

"Go away," screamed Rosamond. "YOU made me fall, you bad woman!"

The woman made no reply, but began to feel her joints, and soon discovered the sprain. Then, in spite of Rosamond's abuse, and the violent pushes and even kicks she gave her, she took the hurt ankle in her hands, and stroked and pressed it, gently kneading it, as it were, with her thumbs, as if coaxing every particle of the muscles into its right place. Nor had she done so long before Rosamond lay still. At length she ceased, and said:—

"Now, my child, you may get up."

"I can't get up, and I'm not your child," cried Rosamond. "Go away."

Without another word the woman left her, took up her burden, and continued her journey.

In a little while Rosamond tried to get up, and not only succeeded, but found she could walk, and, indeed, presently discovered that her ankle and foot also were now perfectly well.

"I wasn't much hurt after all," she said to herself, nor sent a single grateful thought after the poor woman, whom she speedily passed once more upon the road without even a greeting.

Late in the afternoon she came to a spot where the path divided into two, and was taking the one she liked the look of better, when she started at the sound of the poor woman's voice, whom she thought she had left far behind, again calling her. She looked round, and there she was, toiling under her load of heather as before.

"You are taking the wrong turn, child." she cried.

"How can you tell that?" said Rosamond. "You know nothing about where I want to go."

"I know that road will take you where you won't want to go," said the woman.

"I shall know when I get there, then," returned Rosamond, "and no thanks to you."

She set off running. The woman took the other path, and was soon out of sight.

By and by, Rosamond found herself in the midst of a peat-moss—a flat, lonely, dismal, black country. She thought, however, that the road would soon lead her across to the other side of it among the farms, and went on without anxiety. But the stream, which had hitherto been her guide, had now vanished; and when it began to grow dark, Rosamond found that she could no longer distinguish the track. She turned, therefore, but only to find that the same darkness covered it behind as well as before. Still she made the attempt to go back by keeping as direct a line as she could, for the path was straight as an arrow. But she could not see enough even to start her in a line, and she had not gone far before she found herself hemmed in, apparently on every side, by ditches and pools of black, dismal, slimy water. And now it was so dark that she could see nothing more than the gleam of a bit of clear sky now and then in the water. Again and again she stepped knee-deep in black mud, and once tumbled down in the shallow edge of a terrible pool; after which she gave up the attempt to escape the meshes of the watery net, stood still, and began to cry bitterly, despairingly. She saw now that her unreasonable anger had made her foolish as well as rude, and felt that she was justly punished for her wickedness to the poor woman who had been so friendly to her. What would Prince think of her, if he knew? She cast herself on the ground, hungry, and cold, and weary.

Presently, she thought she saw long creatures come heaving out of the black pools. A toad jumped upon her, and she shrieked, and sprang to her feet, and would have run away headlong, when she spied in the distance a faint glimmer. She thought it was a Will-o'-the-wisp. What could he be after? Was he looking for her? She dared not run, lest he should see and pounce upon her. The light came nearer, and grew brighter and larger. Plainly, the little fiend was looking for her—he would torment her. After many twistings and turnings among the pools, it came straight towards her, and she would have shrieked, but that terror made her dumb.

It came nearer and nearer, and lo! it was borne by a dark figure, with a burden on its back: it was the poor woman, and no demon, that was looking for her! She gave a scream of joy, fell down weeping at her feet, and clasped her knees. Then the poor woman threw away her burden, laid down her lantern, took the princess up in her arms, folded her cloak around her, and having taken up her lantern again, carried her slowly and carefully through the midst of the black pools, winding hither and thither. All night long she carried her thus, slowly and wearily, until at length the darkness grew a little thinner, an uncertain hint of light came from the east, and the poor woman, stopping on the brow of a little hill, opened her cloak, and set the princess down.

"I can carry you no farther," she said. "Sit there on the grass till the light comes. I will stand here by you."

Rosamond had been asleep. Now she rubbed her eyes and looked, but it was too dark to see any thing more than that there was a sky over her head. Slowly the light grew, until she could see the form of the poor woman standing in front of her; and as it went on growing, she began to think she had seen her somewhere before, till all at once she thought of the wise woman, and saw it must be she. Then she was so ashamed that she bent down her head, and could look at her no longer. But the poor woman spoke, and the voice was that of the wise woman, and every word went deep into the heart of the princess.

"Rosamond," she said, "all this time, ever since I carried you from your father's palace, I have been doing what I could to make you a lovely creature: ask yourself how far I have succeeded."

All her past story, since she found herself first under the wise woman's cloak, arose, and glided past the inner eyes of the princess, and she saw, and in a measure understood, it all. But she sat with her eyes on the ground, and made no sign.

Then said the wise woman:—

"Below there is the forest which surrounds my house. I am going home. If you pledge to come there to me, I will help you, in a way I could not do now, to be good and lovely. I will wait you there all day, but if you start at once, you may be there long before noon. I shall have your breakfast waiting for you. One thing more: the beasts have not yet all gone home to their holes; but I give you my word, not one will touch you so long as you keep coming nearer to my house."

She ceased. Rosamond sat waiting to hear something more; but nothing came. She looked up; she was alone.

Alone once more! Always being left alone, because she would not yield to what was right! Oh, how safe she had felt under the wise woman's cloak! She had indeed been good to her, and she had in return behaved like one of the hyenas of the awful wood! What a wonderful house it was she lived in! And again all her own story came up into her brain from her repentant heart.

"Why didn't she take me with her?" she said. "I would have gone gladly." And she wept. But her own conscience told her that, in the very middle of her shame and desire to be good, she had returned no answer to the words of the wise woman; she had sat like a tree-stump, and done nothing. She tried to say there was nothing to be done; but she knew at once that she could have told the wise woman she had been very wicked, and asked her to take her with her. Now there was nothing to be done.

"Nothing to be done!" said her conscience. "Cannot you rise, and walk down the hill, and through the wood?"

"But the wild beasts!"

"There it is! You don't believe the wise woman yet! Did she not tell you the beasts would not touch you?"

"But they are so horrid!"

"Yes, they are; but it would be far better to be eaten up alive by them than live on—such a worthless creature as you are. Why, you're not fit to be thought about by any but bad ugly creatures."

This was how herself talked to her.

XII.

All at once she jumped to her feet, and ran at full speed down the hill and into the wood. She heard howlings and yellings on all sides of her, but she ran straight on, as near as she could judge. Her spirits rose as she ran. Suddenly she saw before her, in the dusk of the thick wood, a group of some dozen wolves and hyenas, standing all together right in her way, with their green eyes fixed upon her staring. She faltered one step, then bethought her of what the wise woman had promised, and keeping straight on, dashed right into the middle of them. They fled howling, as if she had struck them with fire. She was no more afraid after that, and ere the sun was up she was out of the wood and upon the heath, which no bad thing could step upon and live. With the first peep of the sun above the horizon, she saw the little cottage before her, and ran as fast as she could run towards it, When she came near it, she saw that the door was open, and ran straight into the outstretched arms of the wise woman.

The wise woman kissed her and stroked her hair, set her down by the fire, and gave her a bowl of bread and milk.

When she had eaten it she drew her before her where she sat, and spoke to her thus:—

"Rosamond, if you would be a blessed creature instead of a mere wretch, you must submit to be tried."

"Is that something terrible?" asked the princess, turning white.

"No, my child; but it is something very difficult to come well out of. Nobody who has not been tried knows how difficult it is; but whoever has come well out of it, and those who do not overcome never do come out of it, always looks back with horror, not on what she has come through, but on the very idea of the possibility of having failed, and being still the same miserable creature as before."

"You will tell me what it is before it begins?" said the princess.

"I will not tell you exactly. But I will tell you some things to help you. One great danger is that perhaps you will think you are in it before it has really begun, and say to yourself, 'Oh! this is really nothing to me. It may be a trial to some, but for me I am sure it is not worth mentioning.' And then, before you know, it will be upon you, and you will fail utterly and shamefully."

"I will be very, very careful," said the princess. "Only don't let me be frightened."

"You shall not be frightened, except it be your own doing. You are already a brave girl, and there is no occasion to try you more that way. I saw how you rushed into the middle of the ugly creatures; and as they ran from you, so will all kinds of evil things, as long as you keep them outside of you, and do not open the cottage of your heart to let them in. I will tell you something more about what you will have to go through.

"Nobody can be a real princess—do not imagine you have yet been any thing more than a mock one—until she is a princess over herself, that is, until, when she finds herself unwilling to do the thing that is right, she makes herself do it. So long as any mood she is in makes her do the thing she will be sorry for when that mood is over, she is a slave, and no princess. A princess is able to do what is right even should she unhappily be in a mood that would make another unable to do it. For instance, if you should be cross and angry, you are not a whit the less bound to be just, yes, kind even—a thing most difficult in such a mood—though ease itself in a good mood, loving and sweet. Whoever does what she is bound to do, be she the dirtiest little girl in the street, is a princess, worshipful, honorable. Nay, more; her might goes farther than she could send it, for if she act so, the evil mood will wither and die, and leave her loving and clean.—Do you understand me, dear Rosamond?"

As she spoke, the wise woman laid her hand on her head and looked—oh, so lovingly!—into her eyes.

"I am not sure," said the princess, humbly.

"Perhaps you will understand me better if I say it just comes to this, that you must NOT DO what is wrong, however much you are inclined to do it, and you must DO what is right, however much you are disinclined to do it."

"I understand that," said the princess.

"I am going, then, to put you in one of the mood-chambers of which I have many in the house. Its mood will come upon you, and you will have to deal with it."

She rose and took her by the hand. The princess trembled a little, but never thought of resisting.

The wise woman led her into the great hall with the pictures, and through a door at the farther end, opening upon another large hall, which was circular, and had doors close to each other all round it. Of these she opened one, pushed the princess gently in, and closed it behind her.

The princess found herself in her old nursery. Her little white rabbit came to meet her in a lumping canter as if his back were going to tumble over his head. Her nurse, in her rocking-chair by the chimney corner, sat just as she had used. The fire burned brightly, and on the table were many of her wonderful toys, on which, however, she now looked with some contempt. Her nurse did not seem at all surprised to see her, any more than if the princess had but just gone from the room and returned again.

"Oh! how different I am from what I used to be!" thought the princess to herself, looking from her toys to her nurse. "The wise woman has done me so much good already! I will go and see mamma at once, and tell her I am very glad to be at home again, and very sorry I was so naughty."

She went towards the door.

"Your queen-mamma, princess, cannot see you now," said her nurse.

"I have yet to learn that it is my part to take orders from a servant," said the princess with temper and dignity.

"I beg your pardon, princess," returned her nurse, politely; "but it is my duty to tell you that your queen-mamma is at this moment engaged. She is alone with her most intimate friend, the Princess of the Frozen Regions."

"I shall see for myself," returned the princess, bridling, and walked to the door.

Now little bunny, leap-frogging near the door, happened that moment to get about her feet, just as she was going to open it, so that she tripped and fell against it, striking her forehead a good blow. She caught up the rabbit in a rage, and, crying, "It is all your fault, you ugly old wretch!" threw it with violence in her nurse's face.

Her nurse caught the rabbit, and held it to her face, as if seeking to sooth its fright. But the rabbit looked very limp and odd, and, to her amazement, Rosamond presently saw that the thing was no rabbit, but a pocket-handkerchief. The next moment she removed it from her face, and Rosamond beheld—not her nurse, but the wise woman—standing on her own hearth, while she herself stood by the door leading from the cottage into the hall.

"First trial a failure," said the wise woman quietly.

Overcome with shame, Rosamond ran to her, fell down on her knees, and hid her face in her dress.

"Need I say any thing?" said the wise woman, stroking her hair.

"No, no," cried the princess. "I am horrid."

"You know now the kind of thing you have to meet: are you ready to try again?"

"MAY I try again?" cried the princess, jumping up. "I'm ready. I do not think I shall fail this time."

"The trial will be harder."

Rosamond drew in her breath, and set her teeth. The wise woman looked at her pitifully, but took her by the hand, led her to the round hall, opened the same door, and closed it after her.

The princess expected to find herself again in the nursery, but in the wise

81

woman's house no one ever has the same trial twice. She was in a beautiful garden, full of blossoming trees and the loveliest roses and lilies. A lake was in the middle of it, with a tiny boat. So delightful was it that Rosamond forgot all about how or why she had come there, and lost herself in the joy of the flowers and the trees and the water. Presently came the shout of a child, merry and glad, and from a clump of tulip trees rushed a lovely little boy, with his arms stretched out to her. She was charmed at the sight, ran to meet him, caught him up in her arms, kissed him, and could hardly let him go again. But the moment she set him down he ran from her towards the lake, looking back as he ran, and crying "Come, come."

She followed. He made straight for the boat, clambered into it, and held out his hand to help her in. Then he caught up the little boat-hook, and pushed away from the shore: there was a great white flower floating a few yards off, and that was the little fellow's goal. But, alas! no sooner had Rosamond caught sight of it, huge and glowing as a harvest moon, than she felt a great desire to have it herself. The boy, however, was in the bows of the boat, and caught it first. It had a long stem, reaching down to the bottom of the water, and for a moment he tugged at it in vain, but at last it gave way so suddenly, that he tumbled back with the flower into the bottom of the boat. Then Rosamond, almost wild at the danger it was in as he struggled to rise, hurried to save it, but somehow between them it came in pieces, and all its petals of fretted silver were scattered about the boat. When the boy got up, and saw the ruin his companion had occasioned, he burst into tears, and having the long stalk of the flower still in his hand, struck her with it across the face. It did not hurt her much, for he was a very little fellow, but it was wet and slimy. She tumbled rather than rushed at him, seized him in her arms, tore him from his frightened grasp, and flung him into the water. His head struck on the boat as he fell, and he sank at once to the bottom, where he lay looking up at her with white face and open eyes.

The moment she saw the consequences of her deed she was filled with horrible dismay. She tried hard to reach down to him through the water, but it was far deeper than it looked, and she could not. Neither could she get her eyes to leave the white face: its eyes fascinated and fixed hers; and there she lay leaning over the boat and staring at the death she had made. But a voice crying, "Ally! Ally!" shot to her heart, and springing to her feet she saw a lovely lady come running down the grass to the brink of the water with her hair flying about her head.

"Where is my Ally?" she shrieked.

But Rosamond could not answer, and only stared at the lady, as she had before stared at her drowned boy.

Then the lady caught sight of the dead thing at the bottom of the water, and rushed in, and, plunging down, struggled and groped until she reached it. Then she rose and stood up with the dead body of her little son in her arms, his head hanging back, and the water streaming from him.

"See what you have made of him, Rosamond!" she said, holding the body out to her; "and this is your second trial, and also a failure."

The dead child melted away from her arms, and there she stood, the wise woman, on her own hearth, while Rosamond found herself beside the little well on the floor of the cottage, with one arm wet up to the shoulder. She threw herself on the heather-bed and wept from relief and vexation both.

The wise woman walked out of the cottage, shut the door, and left her alone. Rosamond was sobbing, so that she did not hear her go. When at length she looked up, and saw that the wise woman was gone, her misery returned afresh and tenfold, and she wept and wailed. The hours passed, the shadows of evening began to fall, and the wise woman entered.

XIII.

She went straight to the bed, and taking Rosamond in her arms, sat down with her by the fire.

"My poor child!" she said. "Two terrible failures! And the more the harder! They get stronger and stronger. What is to be done?"

"Couldn't you help me?" said Rosamond piteously.

"Perhaps I could, now you ask me," answered the wise woman. "When you are ready to try again, we shall see."

"I am very tired of myself," said the princess. "But I can't rest till I try again."

"That is the only way to get rid of your weary, shadowy self, and find your strong, true self. Come, my child; I will help you all I can, for now I CAN help you."

Yet again she led her to the same door, and seemed to the princess to send her yet again alone into the room. She was in a forest, a place half wild, half tended. The trees were grand, and full of the loveliest birds, of all glowing gleaming and radiant colors, which, unlike the brilliant birds we know in our world, sang deliciously, every one according to his color. The trees were not at all crowded, but their leaves were so thick, and their boughs spread so far, that it was only here and there a sunbeam could get straight through. All the gentle creatures of a forest were there, but no creatures that killed, not even a weasel to kill the rabbits, or a beetle to eat the snails out of their striped shells. As to the butterflies, words would but wrong them if they tried to tell how gorgeous they were. The princess's delight was so great that she neither laughed nor ran, but walked about with a solemn countenance and stately step.

"But where are the flowers?" she said to herself at length.

They were nowhere. Neither on the high trees, nor on the few shrubs that grew here and there amongst them, were there any blossoms; and in the grass that grew everywhere there was not a single flower to be seen.

"Ah, well!" said Rosamond again to herself, "where all the birds and butterflies are living flowers, we can do without the other sort."

Still she could not help feeling that flowers were wanted to make the beauty of the forest complete.

Suddenly she came out on a little open glade; and there, on the root of a great oak, sat the loveliest little girl, with her lap full of flowers of all colors, but of such kinds as Rosamond had never before seen. She was playing with them—burying her hands in them, tumbling them about, and every now and then picking one from the rest, and throwing it away. All the time she never smiled, except with her eyes, which were as full as they could hold of the laughter of the spirit—a laughter which in this world is never heard, only sets the eyes alight with a liquid shining. Rosamond drew nearer, for the wonderful creature would have drawn a tiger to her side, and tamed him on the way. A few yards from her, she came upon one of her cast-away flowers and stooped to pick it up, as well she might where none grew save in her own longing. But to her amazement she found, instead of a flower thrown away to wither, one fast rooted and quite at home. She left it, and went to another; but it also was fast in the soil, and growing comfortably in the warm grass. What could it mean? One after another she tried, until at length she was satisfied that it was the same with every flower the little girl threw from her lap.

She watched then until she saw her throw one, and instantly bounded to the spot. But the flower had been quicker than she: there it grew, fast fixed in the earth, and, she thought, looked at her roguishly. Something evil moved in her, and she plucked it.

"Don't! don't!" cried the child. "My flowers cannot live in your hands."

Rosamond looked at the flower. It was withered already. She threw it from her, offended. The child rose, with difficulty keeping her lapful together, picked it up, carried it back, sat down again, spoke to it, kissed it, sang to it—oh! such a sweet, childish little song!—the princess never could recall a word of it—and threw it away. Up rose its little head, and there it was, busy growing again!

Rosamond's bad temper soon gave way: the beauty and sweetness of the child had overcome it; and, anxious to make friends with her, she drew near, and said:

"Won't you give me a little flower, please, you beautiful child?"

"There they are; they are all for you," answered the child, pointing with her outstretched arm and forefinger all round.

"But you told me, a minute ago, not to touch them."

"Yes, indeed, I did."

"They can't be mine, if I'm not to touch them."

"If, to call them yours, you must kill them, then they are not yours, and never, never can be yours. They are nobody's when they are dead."

"But you don't kill them."

"I don't pull them; I throw them away. I live them."

"How is it that you make them grow?"

"I say, 'You darling!' and throw it away and there it is."

"Where do you get them?"

"In my lap."

"I wish you would let me throw one away."

"Have you got any in your lap? Let me see."

"No; I have none."

"Then you can't throw one away, if you haven't got one."

"You are mocking me!" cried the princess.

"I am not mocking you," said the child, looking her full in the face, with reproach in her large blue eyes.

"Oh, that's where the flowers come from!" said the princess to herself, the moment she saw them, hardly knowing what she meant.

Then the child rose as if hurt, and quickly threw away all the flowers she had in her lap, but one by one, and without any sign of anger. When they were all gone, she stood a moment, and then, in a kind of chanting cry, called, two or three times, "Peggy! Peggy! Peggy!"

A low, glad cry, like the whinny of a horse, answered, and, presently, out of the wood on the opposite side of the glade, came gently trotting the loveliest little snow-white pony, with great shining blue wings, half-lifted from his shoulders. Straight towards the little girl, neither hurrying nor lingering, he trotted with light elastic tread.

Rosamond's love for animals broke into a perfect passion of delight at the vision. She rushed to meet the pony with such haste, that, although clearly the best trained animal under the sun, he started back, plunged, reared, and struck out with his fore-feet ere he had time to observe what sort of a creature it was that had so startled him. When he perceived it was a little girl, he dropped instantly upon all fours, and content with avoiding her, resumed his quiet trot in the direction of his mistress. Rosamond stood gazing after him in miserable disappointment.

When he reached the child, he laid his head on her shoulder, and she put her arm up round his neck; and after she had talked to him a little, he turned and came trotting back to the princess.

Almost beside herself with joy, she began caressing him in the rough way which, not-withstanding her love for them, she was in the habit of using with animals; and she was not gentle enough, in herself even, to see that he did not like it, and was only putting up with it for the sake of his mistress. But when, that she might jump upon his back, she laid hold of one of his wings, and ruffled some of the blue feathers, he wheeled suddenly about, gave his long tail a sharp whisk which threw her flat on the grass, and, trotting back

87

to his mistress, bent down his head before her as if asking excuse for ridding himself of the unbearable.

The princess was furious. She had forgotten all her past life up to the time when she first saw the child: her beauty had made her forget, and yet she was now on the very borders of hating her. What she might have done, or rather tried to do, had not Peggy's tail struck her down with such force that for a moment she could not rise, I cannot tell.

But while she lay half-stunned, her eyes fell on a little flower just under them. It stared up in her face like the living thing it was, and she could not take her eyes off its face. It was like a primrose trying to express doubt instead of confidence. It seemed to put her half in mind of something, and she felt as if shame were coming. She put out her hand to pluck it; but the moment her fingers touched it, the flower withered up, and hung as dead on its stalks as if a flame of fire had passed over it.

Then a shudder thrilled through the heart of the princess, and she thought with herself, saying—"What sort of a creature am I that the flowers wither when I touch them, and the ponies despise me with their tails? What a wretched, coarse, ill-bred creature I must be! There is that lovely child giving life instead of death to the flowers, and a moment ago I was hating her! I am made horrid, and I shall be horrid, and I hate myself, and yet I can't help being myself!"

She heard the sound of galloping feet, and there was the pony, with the child seated betwixt his wings, coming straight on at full speed for where she lay.

"I don't care," she said. "They may trample me under their feet if they like. I am tired and sick of myself—a creature at whose touch the flowers wither!"

On came the winged pony. But while yet some distance off, he gave a great bound, spread out his living sails of blue, rose yards and yards above her in the air, and alighted as gently as a bird, just a few feet on the other side of her. The child slipped down and came and kneeled over her.

"Did my pony hurt you?" she said. "I am so sorry!"

"Yes, he hurt me," answered the princess, "but not more than I deserved, for I took liberties with him, and he did not like it."

"Oh, you dear!" said the little girl. "I love you for talking so of my Peggy. He is a good pony, though a little playful sometimes. Would you like a ride upon him?"

"You darling beauty!" cried Rosamond, sobbing. "I do love you so, you are so good. How did you become so sweet?"

"Would you like to ride my pony?" repeated the child, with a heavenly smile in her eyes.

"No, no; he is fit only for you. My clumsy body would hurt him," said Rosamond.

"You don't mind me having such a pony?" said the child.

"What! mind it?" cried Rosamond, almost indignantly. Then remembering certain thoughts that had but a few moments before passed through her mind, she looked on the ground and was silent.

"You don't mind it, then?" repeated the child.

"I am very glad there is such a you and such a pony, and that such a you has got such a pony," said Rosamond, still looking on the ground. "But I do wish the flowers would not die when I touch them. I was cross to see you make them grow, but now I should be content if only I did not make them wither."

As she spoke, she stroked the little girl's bare feet, which were by her, half buried in the soft moss, and as she ended she laid her cheek on them and kissed them.

"Dear princess!" said the little girl, "the flowers will not always wither at your touch. Try now—only do not pluck it. Flowers ought never to be plucked except to give away. Touch it gently."

A silvery flower, something like a snow-drop, grew just within her reach.

Timidly she stretched out her hand and touched it. The flower trembled, but neither shrank nor withered.

"Touch it again," said the child.

It changed color a little, and Rosamond fancied it grew larger.

"Touch it again," said the child.

It opened and grew until it was as large as a narcissus, and changed and deepened in color till it was a red glowing gold.

Rosamond gazed motionless. When the transfiguration of the flower was perfected, she sprang to her feet with clasped hands, but for very ecstasy of joy stood speechless, gazing at the child.

"Did you never see me before, Rosamond?" she asked.

"No, never," answered the princess. "I never saw any thing half so lovely."

"Look at me," said the child.

And as Rosamond looked, the child began, like the flower, to grow larger. Quickly through every gradation of growth she passed, until she stood before her a woman perfectly beautiful, neither old nor young; for hers was the old age of everlasting youth.

Rosamond was utterly enchanted, and stood gazing without word or movement until she could endure no more delight. Then her mind collapsed to the thought—had the pony grown too? She glanced round. There was no pony, no grass, no flowers, no bright-birded forest—but the cottage of the wise woman—and before her, on the hearth of it, the goddess-child, the only thing unchanged.

She gasped with astonishment.

"You must set out for your father's palace immediately," said the lady.

"But where is the wise woman?" asked Rosamond, looking all about.

"Here," said the lady.

And Rosamond, looking again, saw the wise woman, folded as usual in her long dark cloak.

"And it was you all the time?" she cried in delight, and kneeled before her, burying her face in her garments.

"It always is me, all the time," said the wise woman, smiling.

"But which is the real you?" asked Rosamond; "this or that?"

"Or a thousand others?" returned the wise woman. "But the one you have just seen is the likest to the real me that you are able to see just yet—but—. And that me you could not have seen a little while ago.—But, my darling child," she went on, lifting her up and clasping her to her bosom, "you must not think, because you have seen me once, that therefore you are capable of seeing me at all times. No; there are many things in you yet that must be changed before that can be. Now, however, you will seek me. Every time you feel you want me, that is a sign I am wanting you. There are yet many rooms in my house you may have to go through; but when you need no more of them, then you will be able to throw flowers like the little girl you saw in the forest."

The princess gave a sigh.

"Do not think," the wise woman went on, "that the things you have seen in my house are mere empty shows. You do not know, you cannot yet think, how living and true they are.—Now you must go."

She led her once more into the great hall, and there showed her the picture of her father's capital, and his palace with the brazen gates.

"There is your home," she said. "Go to it."

The princess understood, and a flush of shame rose to her forehead. She turned to the wise woman and said:

"Will you forgive ALL my naughtiness, and ALL the trouble I have given you?"

"If I had not forgiven you, I would never have taken the trouble to punish you. If I had not loved you, do you think I would have carried you away in my cloak?"

"How could you love such an ugly, ill-tempered, rude, hateful little wretch?"

"I saw, through it all, what you were going to be," said the wise woman, kissing her. "But remember you have yet only BEGUN to be what I saw."

"I will try to remember," said the princess, holding her cloak, and looking up in her face.

"Go, then," said the wise woman.

Rosamond turned away on the instant, ran to the picture, stepped over the frame of it, heard a door close gently, gave one glance back, saw behind her the loveliest palace-front of alabaster, gleaming in the pale-yellow light of an early summer-morning, looked again to the eastward, saw the faint outline of her father's city against the sky, and ran off to reach it.

It looked much further off now than when it seemed a picture, but the sun was not yet up, and she had the whole of a summer day before her.

XIV.

The soldiers sent out by the king, had no great difficulty in finding Agnes's father and mother, of whom they demanded if they knew any thing of such a young princess as they described. The honest pair told them the truth in every point—that, having lost their own child and found another, they had taken her home, and treated her as their own; that she had indeed called herself a princess, but they had not believed her, because she did not look like one; that, even if they had, they did not know how they could have done differently, seeing they were poor people, who could not afford to keep any idle person about the place; that they had done their best to teach her good ways, and had not parted with her until her bad temper rendered it impossible to put up with her any longer; that, as to the king's proclamation, they heard little of the world's news on their lonely hill, and it had never reached them; that if it had, they did not know how either of them could have gone such a distance from home, and left their sheep or their cottage, one or the other, uncared for.

"You must learn, then, how both of you can go, and your sheep must take care of your cottage," said the lawyer, and commanded the soldiers to bind them hand and foot.

Heedless of their entreaties to be spared such an indignity, the soldiers obeyed, bore them to a cart, and set out for the king's palace, leaving the cottage door open, the fire burning, the pot of potatoes boiling upon it, the sheep scattered over the hill, and the dogs not knowing what to do.

Hardly were they gone, however, before the wise woman walked up, with Prince behind her, peeped into the cottage, locked the door, put the key in her pocket, and then walked away up the hill. In a few minutes there arose a great battle between Prince and the dog which filled his former place—a well-meaning but dull fellow, who could fight better than feed. Prince was not long in showing him that he was meant for his master, and then, by his efforts, and directions to the other dogs, the sheep were soon gathered again, and out of danger from foxes and bad dogs. As soon as this was done, the wise woman left them in charge of Prince, while she went to the next farm to arrange for the folding of the sheep and the feeding of the dogs.

When the soldiers reached the palace, they were ordered to carry their prisoners at once into the presence of the king and queen, in the throne room. Their two thrones stood upon a high dais at one end, and on the floor at the foot of the dais, the soldiers laid their helpless prisoners. The queen commanded that they should be unbound, and ordered them to stand up. They obeyed with the dignity of insulted innocence, and their bearing offended their foolish majesties.

Meantime the princess, after a long day's journey, arrived at the palace, and walked up to the sentry at the gate.

"Stand back," said the sentry.

"I wish to go in, if you please," said the princess gently.

"Ha! ha! ha!" laughed the sentry, for he was one of those dull people who form their judgment from a person's clothes, without even looking in his eyes; and as the princess happened to be in rags, her request was amusing, and the booby thought himself quite clever for laughing at her so thoroughly.

"I am the princess," Rosamond said quietly.

"WHAT princess?" bellowed the man.

"The princess Rosamond. Is there another?" she answered and asked.

But the man was so tickled at the wondrous idea of a princess in rags, that he scarcely heard what she said for laughing. As soon as he recovered a little, he proceeded to chuck the princess under the chin, saying—

"You're a pretty girl, my dear, though you ain't no princess."

Rosamond drew back with dignity.

"You have spoken three untruths at once," she said. "I am NOT pretty, and I AM a princess, and if I were dear to you, as I ought to be, you would not laugh at me because I am badly dressed, but stand aside, and let me go to my father and mother."

The tone of her speech, and the rebuke she gave him, made the man look at her; and looking at her, he began to tremble inside his foolish body, and wonder whether he might not have made a mistake. He raised his hand in salute, and said—

"I beg your pardon, miss, but I have express orders to admit no child whatever within the palace gates. They tell me his majesty the king says he is sick of children."

"He may well be sick of me!" thought the princess; "but it can't mean that he does not want me home again.—I don't think you can very well call me a child," she said, looking the sentry full in the face.

"You ain't very big, miss," answered the soldier, "but so be you say you ain't a child, I'll take the risk. The king can only kill me, and a man must die once."

He opened the gate, stepped aside, and allowed her to pass. Had she lost her temper, as every one but the wise woman would have expected of her, he certainly would not have done so.

She ran into the palace, the door of which had been left open by the porter when he followed the soldiers and prisoners to the throne-room, and bounded up the stairs to look for her father and mother. As she passed the door of the throne-room she heard an unusual noise in it, and running to the king's private entrance, over which hung a heavy curtain, she peeped past the edge of it, and saw, to her amazement, the shepherd and shepherdess standing like culprits before the king and queen, and the same moment heard the king say—

"Peasants, where is the princess Rosamond?"

"Truly, sire, we do not know," answered the shepherd.

"You ought to know," said the king.

"Sire, we could keep her no longer."

"You confess, then," said the king, suppressing the outbreak of the wrath that boiled up in him, "that you turned her out of your house."

For the king had been informed by a swift messenger of all that had passed long before the arrival of the prisoners.

"We did, sire; but not only could we keep her no longer, but we knew not that she was the princess."

"You ought to have known, the moment you cast your eyes upon her," said the king. "Any one who does not know a princess the moment he sees her, ought to have his eyes put out."

"Indeed he ought," said the queen.

To this they returned no answer, for they had none ready.

"Why did you not bring her at once to the palace," pursued the king, "whether you knew her to be a princess or not? My proclamation left nothing to your judgment. It said EVERY CHILD."

"We heard nothing of the proclamation, sire."

"You ought to have heard," said the king. "It is enough that I make proclamations; it is for you to read them. Are they not written in letters of gold upon the brazen gates of this palace?"

"A poor shepherd, your majesty—how often must he leave his flock, and go hundreds of miles to look whether there may not be something in letters of gold upon the brazen gates? We did not know that your majesty had made a proclamation, or even that the princess was lost."

"You ought to have known," said the king.

The shepherd held his peace.

"But," said the queen, taking up the word, "all that is as nothing, when I think how you misused the darling."

The only ground the queen had for saying thus, was what Agnes had told her as to how the princess was dressed; and her condition seemed to the queen so miserable, that she had imagined all sorts of oppression and cruelty.

But this was more than the shepherdess, who had not yet spoken, could bear.

"She would have been dead, and NOT buried, long ago, madam, if I had not carried her home in my two arms."

"Why does she say her TWO arms?" said the king to himself. "Has she more than two? Is there treason in that?"

"You dressed her in cast-off clothes," said the queen.

"I dressed her in my own sweet child's Sunday clothes. And this is what I get for it!" cried the shepherdess, bursting into tears.

"And what did you do with the clothes you took off her? Sell them?"

"Put them in the fire, madam. They were not fit for the poorest child in the mountains. They were so ragged that you could see her skin through them in twenty different places."

"You cruel woman, to torture a mother's feelings so!" cried the queen, and in her turn burst into tears.

"And I'm sure," sobbed the shepherdess, "I took every pains to teach her what it was right for her to know. I taught her to tidy the house and"—

"Tidy the house!" moaned the queen. "My poor wretched offspring!"

"And peel the potatoes, and"—

"Peel the potatoes!" cried the queen. "Oh, horror!"

"And black her master's boots," said the shepherdess.

"Black her master's boots!" shrieked the queen. "Oh, my white-handed princess! Oh, my ruined baby!"

"What I want to know," said the king, paying no heed to this maternal duel, but patting the top of his sceptre as if it had been the hilt of a sword which he was about to draw, "is, where the princess is now."

The shepherd made no answer, for he had nothing to say more than he had said already.

"You have murdered her!" shouted the king. "You shall be tortured till you confess the truth; and then you shall be tortured to death, for you are the most abominable wretches in the whole wide world."

"Who accuses me of crime?" cried the shepherd, indignant.

"I accuse you," said the king; "but you shall see, face to face, the chief witness to your villany. Officer, bring the girl."

Silence filled the hall while they waited. The king's face was swollen with anger. The queen hid hers behind her handkerchief. The shepherd and shepherdess bent their eyes on the ground, wondering. It was with difficulty Rosamond could keep her place, but so wise had she already become that she saw it would be far better to let every thing come out before she interfered.

At length the door opened, and in came the officer, followed by Agnes, looking white as death and mean as sin.

The shepherdess gave a shriek, and darted towards her with arms spread wide; the shepherd followed, but not so eagerly.

"My child! my lost darling! my Agnes!" cried the shepherdess.

"Hold them asunder," shouted the king. "Here is more villany! What! have I a scullery-maid in my house born of such parents? The parents of such a child must be capable of any thing. Take all three of them to the rack. Stretch them till their joints are torn asunder, and give them no water. Away with them!"

The soldiers approached to lay hands on them. But, behold! a girl all in rags, with such a radiant countenance that it was right lovely to see, darted between, and careless of the royal presence, flung herself upon the shepherdess, crying,—

"Do not touch her. She is my good, kind mistress."

But the shepherdess could hear or see no one but her Agnes, and pushed her away. Then the princess turned, with the tears in her eyes, to the shepherd, and threw her arms about his neck and pulled down his head and kissed him. And the tall shepherd lifted her to his bosom and kept her there, but his eyes were fixed on his Agnes.

"What is the meaning of this?" cried the king, starting up from his throne. "How did that ragged girl get in here? Take her away with the rest. She is one of them, too."

But the princess made the shepherd set her down, and before any one could interfere she had run up the steps of the dais and then the steps of the king's throne like a squirrel, flung herself upon the king, and begun to smother him with kisses.

All stood astonished, except the three peasants, who did not even see what took place. The shepherdess kept calling to her Agnes, but she was so ashamed that she did not dare even lift her eyes to meet her mother's, and the shepherd kept gazing on her in silence. As for the king, he was so breathless and aghast with astonishment, that he was too feeble to fling the ragged child from him, as he tried to do. But she left him, and running down the steps of the one throne and up those of the other, began kissing the queen next. But the queen cried out,—

"Get away, you great rude child!—Will nobody take her to the rack?"

Then the princess, hardly knowing what she did for joy that she had come in time, ran down the steps of the throne and the dais, and placing herself between the shepherd and shepherdess, took a hand of each, and stood looking at the king and queen.

Their faces began to change. At last they began to know her. But she was so altered—so lovelily altered, that it was no wonder they should not have known her at the first glance; but it was the fault of the pride and anger and injustice with which their hearts were filled, that they did not know her at the second.

The king gazed and the queen gazed, both half risen from their thrones, and looking as if about to tumble down upon her, if only they could be right sure that the ragged girl was their own child. A mistake would be such a dreadful thing!

"My darling!" at last shrieked the mother, a little doubtfully.

"My pet of pets?" cried the father, with an interrogative twist of tone.

Another moment, and they were half way down the steps of the dais.

"Stop!" said a voice of command from somewhere in the hall, and, king and queen as they were, they stopped at once half way, then drew themselves up, stared, and began to grow angry again, but durst not go farther.

The wise woman was coming slowly up through the crowd that filled the hall. Every one made way for her. She came straight on until she stood in front of the king and queen.

"Miserable man and woman!" she said, in words they alone could hear, "I took your daughter away when she was worthy of such parents; I bring her back, and they are unworthy of her. That you did not know her when she came to you is a small wonder, for you have been blind in soul all your lives: now be blind in body until your better eyes are unsealed."

She threw her cloak open. It fell to the ground, and the radiance that flashed from her robe of snowy whiteness, from her face of awful beauty, and from her eyes that shone like pools of sunlight, smote them blind.

Rosamond saw them give a great start, shudder, waver to and fro, then sit down on the steps of the dais; and she knew they were punished, but knew not how. She rushed up to them, and catching a hand of each said—

"Father, dear father! mother dear! I will ask the wise woman to forgive you."

"Oh, I am blind! I am blind!" they cried together. "Dark as night! Stone blind!"

Rosamond left them, sprang down the steps, and kneeling at her feet, cried, "Oh, my lovely wise woman! do let them see. Do open their eyes, dear, good, wise woman."

The wise woman bent down to her, and said, so that none else could hear, "I will one day. Meanwhile you must be their servant, as I have been yours. Bring them to me, and I will make them welcome."

Rosamond rose, went up the steps again to her father and mother, where they sat like statues with closed eyes, half-way from the top of the dais where stood their empty thrones, seated herself between them, took a hand of each, and was still.

All this time very few in the room saw the wise woman. The moment she threw off her cloak she vanished from the sight of almost all who were present. The woman who swept and dusted the hall and brushed the thrones, saw her, and the shepherd had a glimmering vision of her; but no one else that I know of caught a glimpse of her. The shepherdess did not see her. Nor did Agnes, but she felt her presence upon her like the beat of a furnace seven times heated.

As soon as Rosamond had taken her place between her father and mother, the wise woman lifted her cloak from the floor, and threw it again around her. Then everybody saw her, and Agnes felt as if a soft dewy cloud had come between her and the torrid rays of a vertical sun. The wise woman turned to the shepherd and shepherdess.

"For you," she said, "you are sufficiently punished by the work of your own hands. Instead of making your daughter obey you, you left her to be a slave to herself; you coaxed when you ought to have compelled; you praised when you ought to have been silent; you fondled when you ought to have punished; you threatened when you ought to have inflicted—and there she stands, the full-grown result of your foolishness! She is your crime and your punishment. Take her home with you, and live hour after hour with the pale-hearted disgrace you call your daughter. What she is, the worm at her heart has begun to teach her. When life is no longer endurable, come to me.

"Madam," said the shepherd, "may I not go with you now?"

"You shall," said the wise woman.

"Husband! husband!" cried the shepherdess, "how are we two to get home without you?"

"I will see to that," said the wise woman. "But little of home you will find it until you have come to me. The king carried you hither, and he shall carry you back. But your husband shall not go with you. He cannot now if he would."

The shepherdess looked and saw that the shepherd stood in a deep sleep. She went to him and sought to rouse him, but neither tongue nor hands were of the slightest avail.

The wise woman turned to Rosamond.

"My child," she said, "I shall never be far from you. Come to me when you will. Bring them to me."

Rosamond smiled and kissed her hand, but kept her place by her parents. They also were now in a deep sleep like the shepherd.

The wise woman took the shepherd by the hand, and led him away.

And that is all my double story. How double it is, if you care to know, you must find out. If you think it is not finished—I never knew a story that was. I could tell you a great deal more concerning them all, but I have already told more than is good for those who read but with their foreheads, and enough for those whom it has made look a little solemn, and sigh as they close the book.

CROSS PURPOSES AND THE SHADOWS

CROSS PURPOSES

CHAPTER I.

Once upon a time, the Queen of Fairyland, finding her own subjects far too well-behaved to be amusing, took a sudden longing to have a mortal or two at her Court. So, after looking about her for some time, she fixed upon two to bring to Fairyland.

But how were they to be brought?

"Please your majesty," said at last the daughter of the prime-minister, "I will bring the girl."

The speaker, whose name was Peaseblossom, after her great-great-grandmother, looked so graceful, and hung her head so apologetically, that the Queen said at once,—

"How will you manage it, Peaseblossom?"

"I will open the road before her, and close it behind her."

"I have heard that you have pretty ways of doing things; so you may try."

The court happened to be held in an open forest-glade of smooth turf, upon which there was just one mole-heap. As soon as the Queen had given her permission to Peaseblossom, up through the mole-heap came the head of a goblin, which cried out,—

"Please your majesty, I will bring the boy."

"You!" exclaimed the Queen. "How will you do it?"

The goblin began to wriggle himself out of the earth, as if he had been a snake, and the whole world his skin, till the court was convulsed with laughter. As soon as he got free, he began to roll over and over, in every possible manner, rotatory and cylindrical, all at once, until he reached the wood. The courtiers followed, holding their sides, so that the Queen was left sitting upon her throne in solitary state.

When they reached the wood, the goblin, whose name was Toadstool, was nowhere to be seen. While they were looking for him, out popped his head from the mole-heap again, with the words,—

"So, your majesty."

"You have taken your own time to answer," said the Queen, laughing.

"And my own way too, eh! your majesty?" rejoined Toadstool, grinning.

"No doubt. Well, you may try."

And the goblin, making as much of a bow as he could with only half his neck above ground, disappeared under it.

CHAPTER II.

No mortal, or fairy either, can tell where Fairyland begins and where it ends. But somewhere on the borders of Fairyland there was a nice country village, in which lived some nice country people.

Alice was the daughter of the squire, a pretty, good-natured girl, whom her friends called fairy-like, and others called silly.

One rosy summer evening, when the wall opposite her window was flaked all over with rosiness, she threw herself down on her bed, and lay gazing at the wall. The rose-colour sank through her eyes and dyed her brain, and she began to feel as if she were reading a story-book. She thought she was looking at a western sea, with the waves all red with sunset. But when the colour died out, Alice gave a sigh to see how commonplace the wall grew. "I wish it was always sunset!" she said, half aloud. "I don't like gray things."

"I will take you where the sun is always setting, if you like, Alice," said a sweet, tiny voice near her. She looked down on the coverlet of the bed, and there, looking up at her, stood a lovely little creature. It seemed quite natural that the little lady should be there; for many things we never could believe, have only to happen, and then there is nothing strange about them. She was dressed in white, with a cloak of sunset-red—the colours of the sweetest of sweet-peas. On her head was a crown of twisted tendrils, with a little gold beetle in front.

"Are you a fairy?" said Alice.

"Yes. Will you go with me to the sunset?"

"Yes, I will."

When Alice proceeded to rise, she found that she was no bigger than the fairy; and when she stood up on the counterpane, the bed looked like a great hall with a painted ceiling. As she walked towards Peaseblossom, she stumbled several times over the tufts that made the pattern. But the fairy took her by the hand and led her towards the foot of the bed. Long before they reached it, however, Alice saw that the fairy was a tall, slender lady, and that she herself was quite her own size. What she had taken for tufts on the counterpane were really bushes of furze, and broom, and heather, on the side of a slope.

"Where are we?" asked Alice.

"Going on," answered the fairy.

Alice, not liking the reply, said,—

"I want to go home."

"Good-bye, then!" answered the fairy.

Alice looked round. A wide, hilly country lay all about them. She could not even tell from what quarter they had come.

"I must go with you, I see," she said.

Before they reached the bottom, they were walking over the loveliest meadow-grass. A little stream went cantering down beside them, without channel or bank, sometimes running between the blades, sometimes sweeping the grass all one way under it. And it made a great babbling for such a little stream and such a smooth course.

Gradually the slope grew gentler, and the stream flowed more softly and spread out wider. At length they came to a wood of long, straight poplars, growing out of the water, for the stream ran into the wood, and there stretched out into a lake. Alice thought they could go no farther; but Peaseblossom led her straight on, and they walked through.

It was now dark; but everything under the water gave out a pale, quiet light. There were deep pools here and there, but there was no mud, or frogs, or water-lizards, or eels. All the bottom was pure, lovely grass, brilliantly green. Down the banks of the pools she saw, all under water, primroses and violets and pimpernels. Any flower she wished to see she had only to look for, and she was sure to find it. When a pool came in their way, the fairy swam, and Alice swam by her; and when they got out they were quite dry, though the water was as delightfully wet as water should be. Besides the trees, tall, splendid lilies grew out of it, and hollyhocks and irises and sword-plants, and many other long-stemmed flowers. From every leaf and petal of these, from every branch-tip and tendril, dropped bright water. It gathered slowly at each point, but the points were so many that there was a constant musical plashing of diamond rain upon the still surface of the lake. As they went on, the moon rose and threw a pale mist of light over the whole, and the diamond drops turned to half-liquid pearls, and round every tree-top was a halo of moonlight, and the water went to sleep, and the flowers began to dream.

"Look," said the fairy; "those lilies are just dreaming themselves into a child's sleep. I can see them smiling. This is the place out of which go the things that appear to children every night."

"Is this dreamland, then?" asked Alice.

"If you like," answered the fairy.

"How far am I from home?"

"The farther you go, the nearer home you are."

Then the fairy lady gathered a bundle of poppies and gave it to Alice. The next deep pool that they came to, she told her to throw it in. Alice did so, and following it, laid her head upon it. That moment she began to sink. Down and down she went, till at last she felt herself lying on the long, thick grass at the bottom of the pool, with the poppies under her head and the clear water high over it. Up through it she saw the moon, whose bright face looked sleepy too, disturbed only by the little ripples of the rain from the tall flowers on the edges of the pool.

She fell fast asleep, and all night dreamed about home.

CHAPTER III.

Richard—which is name enough for a fairy story—was the son of a widow in Alice's village. He was so poor that he did not find himself generally welcome; so he hardly went anywhere, but read books at home, and waited upon his mother. His manners, therefore, were shy, and sufficiently awkward to give an unfavourable impression to those who looked at outsides. Alice would have despised him; but he never came near enough for that.

Now Richard had been saving up his few pence in order to buy an umbrella for his mother; for the winter would come, and the one she had was almost torn to ribands. One bright summer evening, when he thought umbrellas must be cheap, he was walking across the market-place to buy one: there, in the middle of it, stood an odd-looking little man, actually selling umbrellas. Here was a chance for him! When he drew nearer, he found that the little man, while vaunting his umbrellas to the skies, was asking such absurdly small prices for them, that no one would venture to buy one. He had opened and laid them all out at full stretch on the market-place—about five-and-twenty of them, stick downwards, like little tents—and he stood beside, haranguing the people. But he would not allow one of the crowd to touch his umbrellas. As soon as his eye fell upon Richard, he changed his tone, and said, "Well, as nobody seems inclined to buy, I think, my dear umbrellas, we had better be going home." Whereupon the umbrellas got up, with some difficulty, and began hobbling away. The people stared at each other with open mouths, for they saw that what they had taken for a lot of umbrellas, was in reality a flock of black geese. A great turkey-cock went gobbling behind them, driving them all down a lane towards the forest. Richard thought with himself, "There is more in this than I can account for. But an umbrella that could lay eggs would be a very jolly umbrella." So by the time the people were beginning to laugh at each other, Richard was half-way down the lane at the heels of the geese. There he stooped and caught one of them, but instead of a goose he had a huge hedgehog in his hands, which he dropped in dismay; whereupon it waddled away a goose as before, and the whole of them began cackling and hissing in a way that he could not mistake. For the turkey-cock, he gobbled and gabbled and choked himself and got right again in the most ridiculous manner. In fact, he seemed sometimes to forget that he was a turkey, and laughed like a fool. All at once, with a simultaneous long-necked hiss, they flew into the wood, and the turkey after them. But Richard soon got up with them again, and found them all hanging by their feet from the trees, in two rows, one on each side of the path, while the turkey was walking on. Him Richard followed; but the moment he reached the middle of the suspended geese, from every side arose the most frightful hisses, and their necks grew longer and longer, till there were nearly thirty broad bills close to his head, blowing in his face, in his ears, and at the back of his neck. But the turkey, looking round and seeing what was going on, turned and walked back. When he reached the place, he looked up at the first and gobbled at him in the wildest manner. That goose grew silent and dropped from the tree. Then he went to the next, and the next, and so on, till he had gobbled them all off the trees, one after another. But when Richard expected to see them go after the turkey, there was nothing there but a flock of huge mushrooms and puff-balls.

"I have had enough of this," thought Richard. "I will go home again."

"Go home, Richard," said a voice close to him.

Looking down, he saw, instead of the turkey, the most comical-looking little man he had ever seen.

"Go home, Master Richard," repeated he, grinning.

"Not for your bidding," answered Richard.

"Come on, then, Master Richard."

"Nor that either, without a good reason."

"I will give you such an umbrella for your mother."

"I don't take presents from strangers."

"Bless you, I'm no stranger here! Oh, no! not at all." And he set off in the manner usual with him, rolling every way at once.

Richard could not help laughing and following. At length Toadstool plumped into a great hole full of water. "Served him right!" thought Richard. "Served him right!" bawled the goblin, crawling out again, and shaking the water from him like a spaniel. "This is the very place I wanted, only I rolled too fast." However, he went on rolling again faster than before, though it was now uphill, till he came to the top of a considerable height, on which grew a number of palm-trees.

"Have you a knife, Richard?" said the goblin, stopping all at once, as if he had been walking quietly along, just like other people.

Richard pulled out a pocket-knife and gave it to the creature, who instantly cut a deep gash in one of the trees. Then he bounded to another and did the same, and so on till he had gashed them all. Richard, following him, saw that a little stream, clearer than the clearest water, began to flow from each, increasing in size the longer it flowed. Before he had reached the last there was quite a tinkling and rustling of the little rills that ran down the

113

stems of the palms. This grew and grew, till Richard saw that a full rivulet was flowing down the side of the hill.

"Here is your knife, Richard," said the goblin; but by the time he had put it in his pocket, the rivulet had grown to a small torrent.

"Now, Richard, come along," said Toadstool, and threw himself into the torrent.

"I would rather have a boat," returned Richard.

"Oh, you stupid!" cried Toadstool crawling up the side of the hill, down which the stream had already carried him some distance.

With every contortion that labour and difficulty could suggest, yet with incredible rapidity, he crawled to the very top of one of the trees, and tore down a huge leaf, which he threw on the ground, and himself after it, rebounding like a ball. He then laid the leaf on the water, held it by the stem, and told Richard to get upon it. He did so. It went down deep in the middle with his weight. Toadstool let it go, and it shot down the stream like an arrow. This began the strangest and most delightful voyage. The stream rushed careering and curveting down the hill-side, bright as a diamond, and soon reached a meadow plain. The goblin rolled alongside of the boat like a bundle of weeds; but Richard rode in triumph through the low grassy country upon the back of his watery steed. It went straight as an arrow, and, strange to tell, was heaped up on the ground, like a ridge of water or a wave, only rushing on endways. It needed no channel, and turned aside for no opposition. It flowed over everything that crossed its path, like a great serpent of water, with folds fitting into all the ups and downs of the way. If a wall came in its course it flowed against it, heaping itself up on itself till it reached the top, whence it plunged to the foot on the other side, and flowed on. Soon he found that it was running gently up a grassy hill. The waves kept curling back as if the wind blew them, or as if they could hardly keep from running down again. But still the stream mounted and flowed, and the waves with it. It found it difficult, but it could do it. When they reached the top, it bore them across a heathy country, rolling over purple heather, and blue harebells, and delicate ferns, and tall foxgloves crowded with bells purple and white. All the time the palm-leaf curled its edges away from the water, and made a delightful boat for Richard, while Toadstool tumbled along in the stream like a porpoise. At length the water began to run very fast, and went faster and faster, till suddenly it plunged them into a deep lake, with a great splash, and stopped there. Toadstool went out of sight, and came up gasping and grinning, while Richard's boat tossed and heaved like a vessel in a storm at sea; but not a drop of water came in. Then the goblin began to swim, and pushed and tugged the boat along. But the lake was so still, and the motion so pleasant, that Richard fell fast asleep.

CHAPTER IV.

When he woke he found himself still afloat upon the broad palm-leaf. He was alone in the middle of a lake, with flowers and trees growing in and out of it everywhere. The sun was just over the tree-tops. A drip of water from the flowers greeted him with music; the mists were dissolving away, and where the sunlight fell on the lake the water was clear as glass. Casting his eyes downward, he saw, just beneath him, far down at the bottom, Alice drowned, as he thought. He was in the act of plunging in, when he saw her open her eyes, and at the same moment begin to float up. He held out his hand, but she repelled it with disdain, and swimming to a tree, sat down on a low branch, wondering how ever the poor widow's son could have found his way into Fairyland. She did not like it. It was an invasion of privilege.

"How did you come here, young Richard?" she asked, from six yards off.

"A goblin brought me."

"Ah! I thought so. A fairy brought me."

"Where is your fairy?"

"Here I am," said Peaseblossom, rising slowly to the surface just by the tree on which Alice was seated.

"Where is your goblin?" retorted Alice.

"Here I am," bawled Toadstool, rushing out of the water like a salmon, and casting a summersault in the air before he fell in again with a tremendous splash. His head rose again close beside Peaseblossom, who being used to such creatures only laughed.

"Isn't he handsome?" he grinned.

"Yes, very. He wants polishing, though."

"You could do that for yourself, you know. Shall we change?"

"I don't mind. You'll find her rather silly."

"That's nothing. The boy's too sensible for me."

He dived, and rose at Alice's feet. She shrieked with terror. The fairy floated away like a water-lily towards Richard. "What a lovely creature!" thought he; but hearing Alice shriek again, he said,

"Don't leave Alice; she's frightened at that queer creature.—I don't think there's any harm in him, though, Alice."

"Oh, no! He won't hurt her," said Peaseblossom. "I'm tired of her. He's going to take her to the court, and I will take you."

"I don't want to go."

"But you must. You can't go home again. You don't know the way."

"Richard! Richard!" cried Alice, in an agony.

Richard sprang from his boat, and was by her side in a moment.

"He pinched me," cried Alice.

Richard hit the goblin a terrible blow on the head; but it took no more effect upon him than if his head had been a round ball of india-rubber. He gave Richard a furious look, however, and bawling out, "You'll repent that, Dick!" vanished under the water.

"Come along, Richard; make haste; he will murder you," cried the fairy.

"It is all your fault," said Richard. "I won't leave Alice."

Then the fairy saw it was all over with her and Toadstool; for they can do nothing with mortals against their will. So she floated away across the water in Richard's boat, holding her robe for a sail, and vanished, leaving the two alone in the lake.

"You have driven away my fairy!" cried Alice. "I shall never get home now. It is all your fault, you naughty young man."

"I drove away the goblin," remonstrated Richard.

"Will you please to sit on the other side of the tree? I wonder what my papa would say if he saw me talking to you!"

"Will you come to the next tree, Alice?" said Richard, after a pause.

Alice, who had been crying all the time that Richard was thinking, said "I won't." Richard, therefore, plunged into the water without her, and swam for the tree. Before he had got half-way, however, he heard Alice crying "Richard! Richard!" This was just what he wanted. So he turned back, and Alice threw herself into the water. With Richard's help she swam pretty well, and they reached the tree. "Now for the next!" said Richard; and they swam to the next, and then to the third. Every tree they reached was larger than the last, and every tree before them was larger still. So they swam from tree to tree, till they came to one that was so large that they could not see round it. What was to be done? Clearly to climb this tree. It was a dreadful prospect for Alice, but Richard proceeded to climb; and by putting her feet where he put his, and now and then getting hold of his ankle, she managed to make her way up. There were a great many stumps where branches had withered off, and the bark was nearly as rough as a hill-side, so there was plenty of foothold for them. When they had climbed a long time, and were getting very tired indeed, Alice cried out, "Richard, I shall drop—I shall. Why did you come this way?" And she began once more to cry. But at that moment Richard caught hold of a branch above his head, and reaching down his other hand got hold of Alice, and held her till she had recovered a little. In a few moments more they reached the fork of the tree, and there they sat and rested. "This is capital!" said Richard, cheerily.

"What is?" asked Alice, sulkily.

"Why, we have room to rest, and there's no hurry for a minute or two. I'm tired."

"You selfish creature!" said Alice. "If you are tired, what must I be!"

"Tired too," answered Richard. "But we've got on bravely. And look! what's that?"

By this time the day was gone, and the night so near, that in the shadows of the tree all was dusky and dim. But there was still light enough to discover that in a niche of the tree sat a huge horned owl, with green spectacles on his beak, and a book in one foot. He took no heed of the intruders, but kept muttering to himself. And what do you think the owl was saying? I will tell you. He was talking about the book that he held upside down in his foot.

"Stupid book this-s-s-s! Nothing in it at all! Everything upside down!

Stupid ass-s-s-s! Says owls can't read! I can read backwards!"

"I think that is the goblin again," said Richard, in a whisper. "However, if you ask a plain question, he must give you a plain answer, for they are not allowed to tell downright lies in Fairyland."

"Don't ask him, Richard; you know you gave him a dreadful blow."

"I gave him what he deserved, and he owes me the same.—Hallo! which is the way out?"

He wouldn't say if you please, because then it would not have been a plain question.

"Down-stairs," hissed the owl, without ever lifting his eyes from the book, which all the time he read upside down, so learned was he.

"On your honour, as a respectable old owl?" asked Richard.

"No," hissed the owl; and Richard was almost sure that he was not really an owl. So he stood staring at him for a few moments, when all at once, without lifting his eyes from the book, the owl said, "I will sing a song," and began:—

"Nobody knows the world but me.

When they're all in bed, I sit up to see

I'm a better student than students all,

For I never read till the darkness fall;

And I never read without my glasses,

And that is how my wisdom passes.

Howlowlwhoolhoolwoolool.

"I can see the wind. Now who can do that?

I see the dreams that he has in his hat;

I see him snorting them out as he goes—

Out at his stupid old trumpet-nose.

Ten thousand things that you couldn't think

I write them down with pen and ink.

Howlowlwhooloolwhitit that's wit.

"You may call it learning—'tis mother-wit.

No one else sees the lady-moon sit

On the sea, her nest, all night, but the owl,

Hatching the boats and the long-legged fowl.

When the oysters gape to sing by rote,

She crams a pearl down each stupid throat.

Howlowlwhitit that's wit, there's a fowl!"

And so singing, he threw the book in Richard's face, spread out his great, silent, soft wings, and sped away into the depths of the tree. When the book struck Richard, he found that it was only a lump of wet moss.

While talking to the owl he had spied a hollow behind one of the branches. Judging this to be the way the owl meant, he went to see, and found a rude, ill-defined staircase going down into the very heart of the trunk. But so large was the tree that this could not have hurt it in the least. Down this stair, then, Richard scrambled as best he could, followed by Alice—not of her own will, she gave him clearly to understand, but because she could do no better. Down, down they went, slipping and falling sometimes, but never very far, because the stair went round and round. It caught Richard when he slipped, and he caught Alice when she did. They had begun to fear that there was no end to the stair, it went round and round so steadily, when, creeping through a crack, they found themselves in a great hall, supported by thousands of pillars of gray stone. Where the little light came from they could not tell. This hall they began to cross in a straight line, hoping to reach one side, and intending to walk along it till they came to some opening. They kept straight by going from pillar to pillar, as they had done before by the trees. Any honest plan will do in Fairyland, if you only stick to it. And no plan will do if you do not stick to it.

It was very silent, and Alice disliked the silence more than the dimness,— so much, indeed, that she longed to hear Richard's voice. But she had always been so cross to him when he had spoken, that he thought it better to let her speak first; and she was too proud to do that. She would not even let him walk alongside of her, but always went slower when he wanted to wait for her; so that at last he strode on alone. And Alice followed. But by degrees the horror of silence grew upon her, and she felt at last as if there was no one in the universe but herself. The hall went on widening around her; their footsteps made no noise; the silence grew so intense that it seemed on the point of taking shape. At last she could bear it no longer. She ran after Richard, got up with him, and laid hold of his arm.

He had been thinking for some time what an obstinate, disagreeable girl Alice was, and wishing he had her safe home to be rid of her, when, feeling a hand, and looking round, he saw that it was the disagreeable girl. She soon began to be companionable after a fashion, for she began to think, putting everything together, that Richard must have been several times in Fairyland before now. "It is very strange," she said to herself; "for he is quite a poor boy, I am sure of that. His arms stick out beyond his jacket like the ribs of his mother's umbrella. And to think of me wandering about Fairyland with him!"

The moment she touched his arm, they saw an arch of blackness before them. They had walked straight to a door—not a very inviting one, for it opened upon an utterly dark passage. Where there was only one door, however, there was no difficulty about choosing. Richard walked straight through it; and from the greater fear of being left behind, Alice faced the lesser fear of going on. In a moment they were in total darkness. Alice clung to Richard's arm, and murmured, almost against her will, "Dear Richard!" It was strange that fear should speak like love; but it was in Fairyland. It was strange, too, that as soon as she spoke thus, Richard should fall in love with her all at once. But what was more curious still was, that, at the same moment, Richard saw her face. In spite of her fear, which had made her pale, she looked very lovely.

"Dear Alice!" said Richard, "how pale you look!"

"How can you tell that, Richard, when all is as black as pitch?"

"I can see your face. It gives out light. Now I see your hands. Now I can see your feet. Yes, I can see every spot where you are going to—No, don't put your foot there. There is an ugly toad just there."

The fact was, that the moment he began to love Alice, his eyes began to send forth light. What he thought came from Alice's face, really came from his eyes. All about her and her path he could see, and every minute saw better; but to his own path he was blind. He could not see his hand when he held it straight before his face, so dark was it. But he could see Alice, and that was better than seeing the way—ever so much.

At length Alice too began to see a face dawning through the darkness. It was Richard's face; but it was far handsomer than when she saw it last. Her eyes had begun to give light too. And she said to herself—"Can it be that I love the poor widow's son?—I suppose that must be it," she answered herself, with a smile; for she was not disgusted with herself at all. Richard saw the smile, and was glad. Her paleness had gone, and a sweet rosiness had taken its place. And now she saw Richard's path as he saw hers, and between the two sights they got on well.

They were now walking on a path betwixt two deep waters, which never moved, shining as black as ebony where the eyelight fell. But they saw ere long that this path kept growing narrower and narrower. At last, to Alice's dismay, the black waters met in front of them.

"What is to be done now, Richard?" she said.

When they fixed their eyes on the water before them, they saw that it was swarming with lizards, and frogs, and black snakes, and all kinds of strange and ugly creatures, especially some that had neither heads, nor tails, nor legs, nor fins, nor feelers, being, in fact, only living lumps. These kept jumping out and in, and sprawling upon the path. Richard thought for a few moments before replying to Alice's question, as, indeed, well he might. But he came to the conclusion that the path could not have gone on for the sake of stopping there; and that it must be a kind of finger that pointed on where it was not allowed to go itself. So he caught up Alice in his strong arms, and jumped into the middle of the horrid swarm. And just as minnows vanish if you throw anything amongst them, just so these wretched creatures vanished, right and left and every way.

He found the water broader than he had expected; and before he got over, he found Alice heavier than he could have believed; but upon a firm, rocky bottom, Richard waded through in safety. When he reached the other side, he found that the bank was a lofty, smooth, perpendicular rock, with some rough steps cut in it. By and by the steps led them right into the rock, and they were in a narrow passage once more, but, this time, leading up. It wound round and round, like the thread of a great screw. At last, Richard knocked his head against something, and could go no farther. The place was close and hot. He put up his hands, and pushed what felt like a warm stone: it moved a little.

"Go down, you brutes!" growled a voice above, quivering with anger. "You'll upset my pot and my cat, and my temper too, if you push that way. Go down!"

Richard knocked very gently, and said: "Please let us out."

"Oh, yes, I dare say! Very fine and soft-spoken! Go down, you goblin brutes! I've had enough of you. I'll scald the hair off your ugly heads if you do that again. Go down, I say!"

Seeing fair speech was of no avail, Richard told Alice to go down a little, out of the way; and, setting his shoulders to one end of the stone, heaved it up; whereupon down came the other end, with a pot, and a fire, and a cat which had been asleep beside it. She frightened Alice dreadfully as she rushed past her, showing nothing but her green lamping eyes.

Richard, peeping up, found that he had turned a hearth-stone upside down. On the edge of the hole stood a little crooked old man, brandishing a mop-stick in a tremendous rage, and hesitating only where to strike him. But Richard put him out of his difficulty by springing up and taking the stick from him. Then, having lifted Alice out, he returned it with a bow, and, heedless of the maledictions of the old man, proceeded to get the stone and the pot up again. For puss, she got out of herself.

Then the old man became a little more friendly, and said: "I beg your pardon, I thought you were goblins. They never will let me alone. But you must allow, it was rather an unusual way of paying a morning call." And the creature bowed conciliatingly.

"It was, indeed," answered Richard. "I wish you had turned the door to us instead of the hearth-stone." For he did not trust the old man. "But," he added, "I hope you will forgive us."

"Oh, certainly, certainly, my dear young people! Use your freedom. But such young people have no business to be out alone. It is against the rules."

"But what is one to do—I mean two to do—when they can't help it?"

"Yes, yes, of course; but now, you know, I must take charge of you. So you sit there, young gentleman; and you sit there, young lady."

He put a chair for one at one side of the hearth, and for the other at the other side, and then drew his chair between them. The cat got upon his hump, and then set up her own. So here was a wall that would let through no moonshine. But although both Richard and Alice were very much amused, they did not like to be parted in this peremptory manner. Still they thought it better not to anger the old man any more—in his own house, too.

But he had been once angered, and that was once too often, for he had made it a rule never to forgive without taking it out in humiliation.

It was so disagreeable to have him sitting there between them, that they felt as if they were far asunder. In order to get the better of the fancy, they wanted to hold each other's hand behind the dwarf's back. But the moment their hands began to approach, the back of the cat began to grow long, and its hump to grow high; and, in a moment more, Richard found himself crawling wearily up a steep hill, whose ridge rose against the stars, while a cold wind blew drearily over it. Not a habitation was in sight; and Alice had vanished from his eyes. He felt, however, that she must be somewhere on the other side, and so climbed and climbed to get over the brow of the hill, and down to where he thought she must be. But the longer he climbed, the farther off the top of the hill seemed; till at last he sank quite exhausted, and—must I confess it?—very nearly began to cry. To think of being separated from Alice all at once, and in such a disagreeable way! But he fell a-thinking instead, and soon said to himself: "This must be some trick of that wretched old man. Either this mountain is a cat or it is not. If it is a mountain, this won't hurt it; if it is a cat, I hope it will." With that, he pulled out his pocket-knife, and feeling for a soft place, drove it at one blow up to the handle in the side of the mountain.

A terrific shriek was the first result; and the second, that Alice and he sat looking at each other across the old man's hump, from which the cat-a-mountain had vanished. Their host sat staring at the blank fireplace, without ever turning round, pretending to know nothing of what had taken place.

"Come along, Alice," said Richard, rising. "This won't do. We won't stop here."

Alice rose at once, and put her hand in his. They walked towards the door. The old man took no notice of them. The moon was shining brightly through the window; but instead of stepping out into the moonlight when they opened the door, they stepped into a great beautiful hall, through the high gothic windows of which the same moon was shining. Out of this hall they could find no way, except by a staircase of stone which led upwards. They ascended it together. At the top Alice let go Richard's hand to peep into a little room, which looked all the colours of the rainbow, just like the inside of a diamond. Richard went a step or two along a corridor, but finding she had left him, turned and looked into the chamber. He could see her nowhere. The room was full of doors; and she must have mistaken the door. He heard her voice calling him, and hurried in the direction of the sound. But he could see nothing of her. "More tricks," he said to himself. "It is of no use to stab this one. I must wait till I see what can be done." Still he heard Alice calling him, and still he followed, as well as he could. At length he came to a doorway, open to the air, through which the moonlight fell. But when he reached it, he found that it was high up in the side of a tower, the wall of which went straight down from his feet, without stair or descent of any kind. Again he heard Alice call him, and lifting his eyes, saw her, across a wide castle-court, standing at another door just like the one he was at, with the moon shining full upon her.

"All right, Alice!" he cried. "Can you hear me?"

"Yes," answered she.

"Then listen. This is all a trick. It is all a lie of that old wretch in the kitchen. Just reach out your hand, Alice dear."

Alice did as Richard asked her; and, although they saw each other many yards off across the court, their hands met.

"There! I thought so!" exclaimed Richard triumphantly. "Now, Alice, I don't believe it is more than a foot or two down to the court below, though it looks like a hundred feet. Keep fast hold of my hand, and jump when I count three." But Alice drew her hand from him in sudden dismay; whereupon Richard said, "Well, I will try first," and jumped. The same moment his cheery laugh came to Alice's ears, and she saw him standing safe on the ground, far below.

"Jump, dear Alice, and I will catch you," said he.

"I can't; I am afraid," answered she.

"The old man is somewhere near you. You had better jump," said Richard.

Alice sprang from the wall in terror, and only fell a foot or two into Richard's arms. The moment she touched the ground, they found themselves outside the door of a little cottage which they knew very well, for it was only just within the wood that bordered on their village. Hand in hand they ran home as fast as they could. When they reached a little gate that led into her father's grounds, Richard bade Alice good-bye. The tears came in her eyes. Richard and she seemed to have grown quite man and woman in Fairyland, and they did not want to part now. But they felt that they must. So Alice ran in the back way, and reached her own room before anyone had missed her. Indeed, the last of the red had not quite faded from the west.

As Richard crossed the market-place on his way home, he saw an umbrella-man just selling the last of his umbrellas. He thought the man gave him a queer look as he passed, and felt very much inclined to punch his head. But remembering how useless it had been to punch the goblin's head, he thought it better not.

In reward of their courage, the Fairy Queen sent them permission to visit Fairyland as often as they pleased; and no goblin or fairy was allowed to interfere with them.

For Peaseblossom and Toadstool, they were both banished from court, and compelled to live together, for seven years, in an old tree that had just one green leaf upon it.

Toadstool did not mind it much, but Peaseblossom did.

THE SHADOWS

Old Ralph Rinkelmann made his living by comic sketches, and all but lost it again by tragic poems. So he was just the man to be chosen king of the fairies, for in Fairyland the sovereignty is elective.

It is no doubt very strange that fairies should desire to have a mortal king; but the fact is, that with all their knowledge and power, they cannot get rid of the feeling that some men are greater than they are, though they can neither fly nor play tricks. So at such times as there happens to be twice the usual number of sensible electors, such a man as Ralph Rinkelmann gets to be chosen.

They did not mean to insist on his residence; for they needed his presence only on special occasions. But they must get hold of him somehow, first of all, in order to make him king. Once he was crowned, they could get him as often as they pleased; but before this ceremony there was a difficulty. For it is only between life and death that the fairies have power over grown-up mortals, and can carry them off to their country. So they had to watch for an opportunity.

Nor had they to wait long. For old Ralph was taken dreadfully ill; and while hovering between life and death, they carried him off, and crowned him king of Fairyland. But after he was crowned, it was no wonder, considering the state of his health, that he should not be able to sit quite upright on the throne of Fairyland; or that, in consequence, all the gnomes and goblins, and ugly, cruel things that live in the holes and corners of the kingdom, should take advantage of his condition, and run quite wild, playing him, king as he was, all sorts of tricks; crowding about his throne, climbing up the steps, and actually scrambling and quarrelling like mice about his ears and eyes, so that he could see and think of nothing else. But I am not going to tell anything more about this part of his adventures just at present. By strong and sustained efforts, he succeeded, after much trouble and suffering, in reducing his rebellious subjects to order. They all vanished to their respective holes and corners; and King Ralph, coming to himself, found himself in his bed, half propped up with pillows.

But the room was full of dark creatures, which gambolled about in the firelight in such a strange, huge, though noiseless fashion, that he thought at first that some of his rebellious goblins had not been subdued with the rest, but had followed him beyond the bounds of Fairyland into his own private house in London. How else could these mad, grotesque hippopotamus-calves make their ugly appearance in Ralph Rinkelmann's bed-room? But he soon found out that although they were like the underground goblins, they were very different as well, and would require quite different treatment. He felt convinced that they were his subjects too, but that he must have overlooked them somehow at his late coronation—if indeed they had been present; for he could not recollect that he had seen anything just like them before. He resolved, therefore, to pay particular attention to their habits, ways, and characters; else he saw plainly that they would soon be too much for him; as indeed this intrusion into his chamber, where Mrs. Rinkelmann, who must be queen if he was king, sat taking some tea by the fireside, evidently foreshadowed. But she, perceiving that he was looking about him with a more composed expression than his face had worn for many days, started up, and came quickly and quietly to his side, and her face was bright with gladness. Whereupon the fire burned up more cheerily; and the figures became more composed and respectful in their behaviour, retreating towards the wall like well-trained attendants. Then the king of Fairyland had some tea and dry toast, and leaning back on his pillows, nearly fell asleep; but not quite, for he still watched the intruders.

Presently the queen left the room to give some of the young princes and princesses their tea; and the fire burned lower, and behold, the figures grew as black and as mad in their gambols as ever! Their favourite games seemed to be Hide and Seek; Touch and Go; Grin and Vanish; and many other such; and all in the king's bed-chamber, too; so that it was quite alarming. It was almost as bad as if the house had been haunted by certain creatures which shall be nameless in a fairy story, because with them Fairyland will not willingly have much to do.

"But it is a mercy that they have their slippers on!" said the king to himself; for his head ached.

As he lay back, with his eyes half shut and half open, too tired to pay longer attention to their games, but, on the whole, considerably more amused than offended with the liberties they took, for they seemed good-natured creatures, and more frolicsome than positively ill-mannered, he became suddenly aware that two of them had stepped forward from the walls, upon which, after the manner of great spiders, most of them preferred sprawling, and now stood in the middle of the floor at the foot of his majesty's bed, becking and bowing and ducking in the most grotesquely obsequious manner; while every now and then they turned solemnly round upon one heel, evidently considering that motion the highest token of homage they could show.

"What do you want?" said the king.

"That it may please your majesty to be better acquainted with us," answered they. "We are your majesty's subjects."

"I know you are. I shall be most happy," answered the king.

"We are not what your majesty takes us for, though. We are not so foolish as your majesty thinks us."

"It is impossible to take you for anything that I know of," rejoined the king, who wished to make them talk, and said whatever came uppermost;—"for soldiers, sailors, or anything: you will not stand still long enough. I suppose you really belong to the fire brigade; at least, you keep putting its light out."

"Don't jest, please your majesty." And as they said the words—for they both spoke at once throughout the interview—they performed a grave somerset towards the king.

"Not jest!" retorted he; "and with you? Why, you do nothing but jest. What are you?"

"The Shadows, sire. And when we do jest, sire, we always jest in earnest. But perhaps your majesty does not see us distinctly."

"I see you perfectly well," returned the king.

"Permit me, however," rejoined one of the Shadows; and as he spoke he approached the king; and lifting a dark forefinger, he drew it lightly but carefully across the ridge of his forehead, from temple to temple. The king felt the soft gliding touch go, like water, into every hollow, and over the top of every height of that mountain-chain of thought. He had involuntarily closed his eyes during the operation, and when he unclosed them again, as soon as the finger was withdrawn, he found that they were opened in more senses than one. The room appeared to have extended itself on all sides, till he could not exactly see where the walls were; and all about it stood the

Shadows motionless. They were tall and solemn; rather awful, indeed, in their appearance, notwithstanding many remarkable traits of grotesqueness, for they looked just like the pictures of Puritans drawn by Cavaliers, with long arms, and very long, thin legs, from which hung large loose feet, while in their countenances length of chin and nose predominated. The solemnity of their mien, however, overcame all the oddity of their form, so that they were very eerie indeed to look at, dressed as they all were in funereal black. But a single glance was all that the king was allowed to have; for the former operator waved his dusky palm across his vision, and once more the king saw only the fire-lighted walls, and dark shapes flickering about upon them. The two who had spoken for the rest seemed likewise to have vanished. But at last the king discovered them, standing one on each side of the fireplace. They kept close to the chimney-wall, and talked to each other across the length of the chimney-piece; thus avoiding the direct rays of the fire, which, though light is necessary to their appearing to human eyes, do not agree with them at all—much less give birth to them, as the king was soon to learn. After a few minutes they again approached the bed, and spoke thus:—

"It is now getting dark, please your majesty. We mean, out of doors in the snow. Your majesty may see, from where he is lying, the cold light of its great winding-sheet—a famous carpet for the Shadows to dance upon, your majesty. All our brothers and sisters will be at church now, before going to their night's work."

"Do they always go to church before they go to work?"

"They always go to church first."

"Where is the church?"

"In Iceland. Would your majesty like to see it?"

"How can I go and see it, when, as you know very well, I am ill in bed? Besides, I should be sure to take cold in a frosty night like this, even if I put on the blankets, and took the feather-bed for a muff."

A sort of quivering passed over their faces, which seemed to be their mode of laughing. The whole shape of the face shook and fluctuated as if it had been some dark fluid; till by slow degrees of gathering calm, it settled into its former rest. Then one of them drew aside the curtains of the bed, and the window-curtains not having been yet drawn, the king beheld the white glimmering night outside, struggling with the heaps of darkness that tried to quench it; and the heavens full of stars, flashing and sparkling like live jewels. The other Shadow went towards the fire and vanished in it.

Scores of Shadows immediately began an insane dance all about the room; disappearing, one after the other, through the uncovered window, and gliding darkly away over the face of the white snow; for the window looked at once on a field of snow. In a few moments, the room was quite cleared of them; but instead of being relieved by their absence, the king felt immediately as if he were in a dead-house, and could hardly breathe for the sense of emptiness and desolation that fell upon him. But as he lay looking out on the snow, which stretched blank and wide before him, he spied in the distance a long dark line which drew nearer and nearer, and showed itself at last to be all the Shadows, walking in a double row, and carrying in the midst of them something like a bier. They vanished under the window, but soon reappeared, having somehow climbed up the wall of the house; for they entered in perfect order by the window, as if melting through the transparency of the glass.

They still carried the bier or litter. It was covered with richest furs, and skins of gorgeous wild beasts, whose eyes were replaced by sapphires and emeralds, that glittered and gleamed in the fire and snow light. The outermost skin sparkled with frost, but the inside ones were soft and warm and dry as the down under a swan's wing. The Shadows approached the bed, and set the litter upon it. Then a number of them brought a huge fur robe, and wrapping it round the king, laid him on the litter in the midst of the furs. Nothing could be more gentle and respectful than the way in which they moved him; and he never thought of refusing to go. Then they put something on his head, and, lifting the litter, carried him once round the room, to fall into order. As he passed the mirror he saw that he was covered with royal ermine, and that his head wore a wonderful crown of gold, set with none but red stones: rubies and carbuncles and garnets, and others whose names he could not tell, glowed gloriously around his head, like the salamandrine essence of all the Christmas fires over the world. A sceptre lay beside him—a rod of ebony, surmounted by a cone-shaped diamond, which, cut in a hundred facets, flashed all the hues of the rainbow, and threw coloured gleams on every side, that looked like Shadows too, but more ethereal than those that bore him. Then the Shadows rose gently to the window, passed through it, and sinking slowing upon the field of outstretched snow, commenced an orderly gliding rather than march along the frozen surface. They took it by turns to bear the king, as they sped with the swiftness of thought, in a straight line towards the north. The pole-star rose above their heads with visible rapidity; for indeed they moved quite as fast as sad thoughts, though not with all the speed of happy desires. England and Scotland slid past the litter of the king of the Shadows. Over rivers and lakes they skimmed and glided. They climbed the high mountains, and crossed the valleys with a fearless bound; till they came to John-o'-Groat's house and the Northern Sea. The sea was not frozen; for all the stars shone as clear out of the deeps below as they shone out of the deeps above; and as the bearers slid along the blue-gray surface, with never a furrow in their track, so pure was the water beneath that the king saw neither surface, bottom, nor substance to it, and seemed to be gliding only through the blue sphere of heaven, with the stars above him, and the stars below him, and between the stars and him nothing but an emptiness, where, for the first time in his life, his soul felt that it had room enough.

At length they reached the rocky shores of Iceland. There they landed, still pursuing their journey. All this time the king felt no cold; for the red stones in his crown kept him warm, and the emerald and sapphire eyes of the wild beasts kept the frosts from settling upon his litter.

Oftentimes upon their way they had to pass through forests, caverns, and rock-shadowed paths, where it was so dark that at first the king feared he should lose his Shadows altogether. But as soon as they entered such places, the diamond in his sceptre began to shine and glow, and flash, sending out streams of light of all the colours that painter's soul could dream of; in which light the Shadows grew livelier and stronger than ever, speeding through the dark ways with an all but blinding swiftness. In the light of the diamond, too, some of their forms became more simple and human, while others seemed only to break out into a yet more untamable absurdity. Once, as they passed through a cave, the king actually saw some of their eyes—strange shadow-eyes; he had never seen any of their eyes before. But at the same moment when he saw their eyes, he knew their faces too, for they turned them full upon him for an instant; and the other Shadows, catching sight of these, shrank and shivered, and nearly vanished. Lovely faces they were; but the king was very thoughtful after he saw them, and continued rather troubled all the rest of the journey. He could not account for those faces being there, and the faces of Shadows, too, with living eyes.

But he soon found that amongst the Shadows a man must learn never to be surprised at anything; for if he does not, he will soon grow quite stupid, in consequence of the endless recurrence of surprises.

At last they climbed up the bed of a little stream, and then, passing through a narrow rocky defile, came out suddenly upon the side of a mountain, overlooking a blue frozen lake in the very heart of mighty hills. Overhead, the aurora borealis was shivering and flashing like a battle of ten thousand spears. Underneath, its beams passed faintly over the blue ice and the sides of the snow-clad mountains, whose tops shot up like huge icicles all about, with here and there a star sparkling on the very tip of one. But as the northern lights in the sky above, so wavered and quivered, and shot hither and thither, the Shadows on the surface of the lake below; now gathering in groups, and now shivering asunder; now covering the whole surface of the lake, and anon condensed into one dark knot in the centre. Every here and there on the white mountains might be seen two or three shooting away towards the tops, to vanish beyond them, so that their number was gradually, though not visibly, diminishing.

"Please your majesty," said the Shadows, "this is our church—the Church of the Shadows."

And so saying, the king's body-guard set down the litter upon a rock, and plunged into the multitudes below. They soon returned, however, and bore the king down into the middle of the lake. All the Shadows came crowding round him, respectfully but fearlessly; and sure never such a grotesque assembly revealed itself before to mortal eyes. The king had seen all kind of gnomes, goblins, and kobolds at his coronation; but they were quite rectilinear figures compared with the insane lawlessness of form in which the Shadows rejoiced; and the wildest gambols of the former were orderly dances of ceremony beside the apparently aimless and wilful contortions of figure, and metamorphoses of shape, in which the latter indulged. They retained, however, all the time, to the surprise of the king, an identity, each of his own type, inexplicably perceptible through every change. Indeed this preservation of the primary idea of each form was more wonderful than the bewildering and ridiculous alterations to which the form itself was every moment subjected.

"What are you?" said the king, leaning on his elbow, and looking around him.

"The Shadows, your majesty," answered several voices at once.

"What Shadows?"

"The human Shadows. The Shadows of men, and women, and their children."

"Are you not the shadows of chairs and tables, and pokers and tongs, just as well?"

At this question a strange jarring commotion went through the assembly with a shock. Several of the figures shot up as high as the aurora, but instantly settled down again to human size, as if overmastering their feelings, out of respect to him who had roused them. One who had bounded to the highest visible icy peak, and as suddenly returned, now elbowed his way through the rest, and made himself spokesman for them during the remaining part of the dialogue.

"Excuse our agitation, your majesty," said he. "I see your majesty has not yet thought proper to make himself acquainted with our nature and habits."

"I wish to do so now," replied the king.

"We are the Shadows," repeated the Shadow solemnly.

"Well?" said the king.

"We do not often appear to men."

"Ha!" said the king.

"We do not belong to the sunshine at all. We go through it unseen, and only by a passing chill do men recognize an unknown presence."

"Ha!" said the king again.

"It is only in the twilight of the fire, or when one man or woman is alone with a single candle, or when any number of people are all feeling the same thing at once, making them one, that we show ourselves, and the truth of things."

"Can that be true that loves the night?" said the king.

"The darkness is the nurse of light," answered the Shadow.

"Can that be true which mocks at forms?" said the king.

"Truth rides abroad in shapeless storms," answered the Shadow.

"Ha! ha!" thought Ralph Rinkelmann, "it rhymes. The Shadow caps my questions with his answers. Very strange!" And he grew thoughtful again.

The Shadow was the first to resume.

"Please your majesty, may we present our petition?"

"By all means," replied the king. "I am not well enough to receive it in proper state."

"Never mind, your majesty. We do not care for much ceremony; and indeed none of us are quite well at present. The subject of our petition weighs upon us."

"Go on," said the king.

"Sire," began the Shadow, "our very existence is in danger. The various sorts of artificial light, both in houses and in men, women, and children, threaten to end our being. The use and the disposition of gaslights, especially high in the centres, blind the eyes by which alone we can be perceived. We are all but banished from towns. We are driven into villages and lonely houses, chiefly old farm-houses, out of which, even, our friends the fairies are fast disappearing. We therefore petition our king, by the power of his art, to restore us to our rights in the house itself, and in the hearts of its inhabitants."

"But," said the king, "you frighten the children."

"Very seldom, your majesty; and then only for their good. We seldom seek to frighten anybody. We mostly want to make people silent and thoughtful; to awe them a little, your majesty."

"You are much more likely to make them laugh," said the king.

"Are we?" said the Shadow.

And approaching the king one step, he stood quite still for a moment. The diamond of the king's sceptre shot out a vivid flame of violet light, and the king stared at the Shadow in silence, and his lip quivered. He never told what he saw then; but he would say:

"Just fancy what it might be if some flitting thoughts were to persist in staying to be looked at."

"It is only," resumed the Shadow, "when our thoughts are not fixed upon any particular object, that our bodies are subject to all the vagaries of elemental influences. Generally, amongst worldly men and frivolous women, we only attach ourselves to some article of furniture or of dress; and they never doubt that we are mere foolish and vague results of the dashing of the waves of the light against the solid forms of which their houses are full. We do not care to tell them the truth, for they would never see it. But let the worldly man—or the frivolous woman—and then—"

At each of the pauses indicated, the mass of Shadows throbbed and heaved with emotion; but they soon settled again into comparative stillness. Once more the Shadow addressed himself to speak. But suddenly they all looked up, and the king, following their gaze, saw that the aurora had begun to pale.

"The moon is rising," said the Shadow. "As soon as she looks over the mountains into the valley, we must be gone, for we have plenty to do by the moon; we are powerful in her light. But if your majesty will come here to-morrow night, your majesty may learn a great deal more about us, and judge for himself whether it be fit to accord our petition; for then will be our grand annual assembly, in which we report to our chiefs the things we have attempted, and the good or bad success we have had."

"If you send for me," returned the king, "I will come."

Ere the Shadow could reply, the tip of the moon's crescent horn peeped up from behind an icy pinnacle, and one slender ray fell on the lake. It shone upon no Shadows. Ere the eye of the king could again seek the earth after beholding the first brightness of the moon's resurrection, they had vanished; and the surface of the lake glittered gold and blue in the pale moonlight.

There the king lay, alone in the midst of the frozen lake, with the moon staring at him. But at length he heard from somewhere a voice that he knew.

"Will you take another cup of tea, dear?" said Mrs. Rinkelmann.

And Ralph, coming slowly to himself, found that he was lying in his own bed.

"Yes, I will," he answered; "and rather a large piece of toast, if you please; for I have been a long journey since I saw you last."

"He has not come to himself quite," said Mrs. Rinkelmann, between her and herself.

"You would be rather surprised," continued Ralph, "if I told you where I had been."

"I dare say I should," responded his wife.

"Then I will tell you," rejoined Ralph.

But at that moment, a great Shadow bounced out of the fire with a single huge leap, and covered the whole room. Then it settled in one corner, and Ralph saw it shaking its fist at him from the end of a preposterous arm. So he took the hint, and held his peace. And it was as well for him. For I happen to know something about the Shadows too; and I know that if he had told his wife all about it just then, they would not have sent for him the following evening.

But as the king, after finishing his tea and toast, lay and looked about him, the Shadows dancing in his room seemed to him odder and more inexplicable than ever. The whole chamber was full of mystery. So it generally was, but now it was more mysterious than ever. After all that he had seen in the Shadow-church, his own room and its Shadows were yet more wonderful and unintelligible than those.

This made it the more likely that he had seen a true vision; for instead of making common things look commonplace, as a false vision would have done, it had made common things disclose the wonderful that was in them.

"The same applies to all arts as well," thought Ralph Rinkelmann.

The next afternoon, as the twilight was growing dusky, the king lay wondering whether or not the Shadows would fetch him again. He wanted very much to go, for he had enjoyed the journey exceedingly, and he longed, besides, to hear some of the Shadows tell their stories. But the darkness grew deeper and deeper, and the shadows did not come. The cause was, that Mrs. Rinkelmann sat by the fire in the gloaming; and they could not carry off the king while she was there. Some of them tried to frighten her away by playing the oddest pranks on the walls, and floor, and ceiling; but altogether without effect; the queen only smiled, for she had a good conscience. Suddenly, however, a dreadful scream was heard from the nursery, and Mrs. Rinkelmann rushed upstairs to see what was the matter. No sooner had she gone than the two warders of the chimney-corners stepped out into the middle of the room, and said, in a low voice,—

"Is your majesty ready?"

"Have you no hearts?" said the king; "or are they as black as your faces? Did you not hear the child scream? I must know what is the matter with her before I go."

"Your majesty may keep his mind easy on that point," replied the warders. "We had tried everything we could think of to get rid of her majesty the queen, but without effect. So a young madcap Shadow, half against the will of the older ones of us, slipped upstairs into the nursery; and has, no doubt, succeeded in appalling the baby, for he is very lithe and long-legged.—

Now, your majesty."

"I will have no such tricks played in my nursery," said the king, rather angrily. "You might put the child beside itself."

"Then there would be twins, your majesty. And we rather like twins."

"None of your miserable jesting! You might put the child out of her wits."

"Impossible, sire; for she has not got into them yet."

"Go away," said the king.

"Forgive us, your majesty. Really, it will do the child good; for that Shadow will, all her life, be to her a symbol of what is ugly and bad. When she feels in danger of hating or envying anyone, that Shadow will come back to her mind and make her shudder."

"Very well," said the king. "I like that. Let us go."

The Shadows went through the same ceremonies and preparations as before; during which, the young Shadow before-mentioned contrived to make such grimaces as kept the baby in terror, and the queen in the nursery, till all was ready. Then with a bound that doubled him up against the ceiling, and a kick of his legs six feet out behind him, he vanished through the nursery door, and reached the king's bed-chamber just in time to take his place with the last who were melting through the window in the rear of the litter, and settling down upon the snow beneath. Away they went as before, a gliding blackness over the white carpet. And it was Christmas-eve.

When they came in sight of the mountain-lake, the king saw that it was crowded over its whole surface with a changeful intermingling of Shadows. They were all talking and listening alternately, in pairs, trios, and groups of every size. Here and there large companies were absorbed in attention to one elevated above the rest, not in a pulpit, or on a platform, but on the stilts of his own legs, elongated for the nonce. The aurora, right overhead, lighted up the lake and the sides of the mountains, by sending down from the zenith, nearly to the surface of the lake, great folded vapours, luminous with all the colours of a faint rainbow.

Many, however, as the words were that passed on all sides, not a shadow of a sound reached the ears of the king: the shadow-speech could not enter his corporeal organs. One of his guides, however, seeing that the king wanted to hear and could not, went through a strange manipulation of his head and ears; after which he could hear perfectly, though still only the voice to which, for the time, he directed his attention. This, however, was a great advantage, and one which the king longed to carry back with him to the world of men.

The king now discovered that this was not merely the church of the Shadows, but their news exchange at the same time. For, as the shadows have no writing or printing, the only way in which they can make each other acquainted with their doings and thinkings, is to meet and talk at this word-mart and parliament of shades. And as, in the world, people read their favourite authors, and listen to their favourite speakers, so here the Shadows seek their favourite Shadows, listen to their adventures, and hear generally what they have to say.

Feeling quite strong, the king rose and walked about amongst them, wrapped in his ermine robe, with his red crown on his head, and his diamond sceptre in his hand. Every group of Shadows to which he drew near, ceased talking as soon as they saw him approach; but at a nod they went on again directly, conversing and relating and commenting, as if no one was there of other kind or of higher rank than themselves. So the king heard a good many stories. At some of them he laughed, and at some of them he cried. But if the stories that the Shadows told were printed, they would make a book that no publisher could produce fast enough to satisfy the buyers. I will record some of the things that the king heard, for he told them to me soon after. In fact, I was for some time his private secretary.

"I made him confess before a week was over," said a gloomy old Shadow.

"But what was the good of that?" rejoined a pert young one. "That could not undo what was done."

"Yes, it could."

"What! bring the dead to life?"

"No; but comfort the murderer. I could not bear to see the pitiable misery he was in. He was far happier with the rope round his neck, than he was with the purse in his pocket. I saved him from killing himself too."

"How did you make him confess?"

"Only by wallowing on the wall a little."

"How could that make him tell?"

"He knows."

The Shadow was silent; and the king turned to another, who was preparing to speak.

"I made a fashionable mother repent."

"How?" broke from several voices, in whose sound was mingled a touch of incredulity.

"Only by making a little coffin on the wall," was the reply.

"Did the fashionable mother confess too?"

"She had nothing more to confess than everybody knew."

"What did everybody know then?"

"That she might have been kissing a living child, when she followed a dead one to the grave.—The next will fare better."

"I put a stop to a wedding," said another.

"Horrid shade!" remarked a poetic imp.

"How?" said others. "Tell us how."

"Only by throwing a darkness, as if from the branch of a sconce, over the forehead of a fair girl.—They are not married yet, and I do not think they will be. But I loved the youth who loved her. How he started! It was a revelation to him."

"But did it not deceive him?"

"Quite the contrary."

"But it was only a shadow from the outside, not a shadow coming through from the soul of the girl."

"Yes. You may say so. But it was all that was wanted to make the meaning of her forehead manifest—yes, of her whole face, which had now and then, in the pauses of his passion, perplexed the youth. All of it, curled nostrils, pouting lips, projecting chin, instantly fell into harmony with that darkness between her eyebrows. The youth understood it in a moment, and went home miserable. And they're not married yet."

"I caught a toper alone, over his magnum of port," said a very dark Shadow; "and didn't I give it him! I made delirium tremens first; and then I settled into a funeral, passing slowly along the length of the opposite wall. I gave him plenty of plumes and mourning coaches. And then I gave him a funeral service, but I could not manage to make the surplice white, which was all the better for such a sinner. The wretch stared till his face passed from purple to grey, and actually left his fifth glass only, unfinished, and took refuge with his wife and children in the drawing-room, much to their surprise. I believe he actually drank a cup of tea; and although I have often looked in since, I have never caught him again, drinking alone at least."

"But does he drink less? Have you done him any good?"

"I hope so; but I am sorry to say I can't feel sure about it."

"Humph! Humph! Humph!" grunted various shadow throats.

"I had such fun once!" cried another. "I made such game of a young clergyman!"

"You have no right to make game of anyone."

"Oh yes, I have—when it is for his good. He used to study his sermons—where do you think?"

"In his study, of course. Where else should it be?"

"Yes and no. Guess again."

"Out amongst the faces in the streets."

"Guess again."

"In still green places in the country?"

"Guess again."

"In old books?"

"Guess again."

"No, no. Tell us."

"In the looking glass. Ha! ha! ha!"

"He was fair game; fair shadow game."

"I thought so. And I made such fun of him one night on the wall! He had sense enough to see that it was himself, and very like an ape. So he got ashamed, turned the mirror with its face to the wall, and thought a little more about his people, and a little less about himself. I was very glad; for, please your majesty,"—and here the speaker turned towards the king—"we don't like the creatures that live in the mirrors. You call them ghosts, don't you?"

Before the king could reply, another had commenced. But the story about the clergyman had made the king wish to hear one of the shadow-sermons. So he turned him towards a long Shadow, who was preaching to a very quiet and listening crowd. He was just concluding his sermon.

"Therefore, dear Shadows, it is the more needful that we love one another as much as we can, because that is not much. We have no such excuse for not loving as mortals have, for we do not die like them. I suppose it is the thought of that death that makes them hate so much. Then again, we go to sleep all day, most of us, and not in the night, as men do. And you know that we forget everything that happened the night before; therefore, we ought to love well, for the love is short. Ah! dear Shadow, whom I love now with all my shadowy soul, I shall not love thee to-morrow eve, I shall not know thee; I shall pass thee in the crowd and never dream that the Shadow whom I now love is near me then. Happy Shades! for we only remember our tales until we have told them here, and then they vanish in the shadow-churchyard, where we bury only our dead selves. Ah! brethren, who would be a man and remember? Who would be a man and weep? We ought indeed to love one another, for we alone inherit oblivion; we alone are renewed with eternal birth; we alone have no gathered weight of years. I will tell you the awful fate of one Shadow who rebelled against his nature, and sought to remember the past. He said, 'I will remember this eve.' He fought with the genial influences of kindly sleep when the sun rose on the awful dead day of light; and although he could not keep quite awake, he dreamed of the foregone eve, and he never forgot his dream. Then he tried again the next night, and the next, and the next; and he tempted another Shadow to try it with him. But at last their awful fate overtook them; for, instead of continuing to be Shadows, they began to cast shadows, as foolish men say; and so they thickened and thickened till they vanished out of our world. They are now condemned to walk the earth, a man and a woman, with death behind them, and memories within them. Ah, brother Shades! let us love one another, for we shall soon forget. We are not men, but Shadows."

The king turned away, and pitied the poor Shadows far more than they pitied men.

"Oh! how we played with a musician one night!" exclaimed a Shadow in another group, to which the king had first directed a passing thought, and then had stopped to listen.—"Up and down we went, like the hammers and dampers on his piano. But he took his revenge on us. For after he had watched us for half an hour in the twilight, he rose and went to his instrument, and played a shadow-dance that fixed us all in sound for ever. Each could tell the very notes meant for him; and as long as he played, we could not stop, but went on dancing and dancing after the music, just as the magician—I mean the musician—pleased. And he punished us well; for he nearly danced us all off our legs and out of shape into tired heaps of collapsed and palpitating darkness. We won't go near him for some time again, if we can only remember it. He had been very miserable all day, he was so poor; and we could not think of any way of comforting him except making him laugh. We did not succeed, with our wildest efforts; but it turned out better than we had expected, after all; for his shadow-dance got him into notice, and he is quite popular now, and making money fast.—If he does not take care, we shall have other work to do with him by and by, poor fellow!"

"I and some others did the same for a poor play-writer once. He had a Christmas piece to write, and [not] being an original genius, it was not so easy for him to find a subject as it is for most of his class. I saw the trouble he was in, and collecting a few stray Shadows, we acted, in dumb-show of course, the funniest bit of nonsense we could think of; and it was quite successful. The poor fellow watched every motion, roaring with laughter at us, and delight at the ideas we put into his head. He turned it all into words, and scenes, and actions; and the piece came off with a splendid success."

"But how long we have to look for a chance of doing anything worth doing," said a long, thin, especially lugubrious Shadow. "I have only done one thing worth telling ever since we met last. But I am proud of that."

"What was it? What was it?" rose from twenty voices.

"I crept into a dining-room, one twilight, soon after Christmas-day. I had been drawn thither by the glow of a bright fire shining through red window-curtains. At first I thought there was no one there, and was on the point of leaving the room, and going out again into the snowy street, when I suddenly caught the sparkle of eyes. I found that they belonged to a little boy who lay very still on a sofa. I crept into a dark corner by the sideboard, and watched him. He seemed very sad, and did nothing but stare into the fire. At last he sighed out,—'I wish mamma would come home.' 'Poor boy!' thought I, 'there is no help for that but mamma.' Yet I would try to while away the time for him. So out of my corner I stretched a long shadow arm, reaching all across the ceiling, and pretended to make a grab at him. He was rather frightened at first; but he was a brave boy, and soon saw that it was all a joke. So when I did it again, he made a clutch at me; and then we had such fun! For though he often sighed and wished mamma would come home, he always began again with me; and on we went with the wildest games. At last his mother's knock came to the door, and starting up in delight, he rushed into the hall to meet her, and forgot all about poor black me. But I did not mind that in the least; for when I glided out after him into the hall, I was well repaid for my trouble by hearing his mother say to him,—'Why, Charlie, my dear, you look ever so much better since I left you!' At that moment I slipped through the closing door, and as I ran across the snow, I heard the mother say,—'What shadow can that be, passing so quickly?' And Charlie answered with a merry laugh,—'Oh! mamma, I suppose it must be the funny shadow that has been playing such games with me all the time you were out.' As soon as the door was shut, I crept along the wall and looked in at the dining-room window. And I heard his mamma say, as she led him into the room, 'What an imagination the boy has!' Ha! ha! ha! Then she looked at him, and the tears came in her eyes; and she stooped down over him, and I heard the sounds of a mingling kiss and sob."

"I always look for nurseries full of children," said another; "and this winter I have been very fortunate. I am sure children belong especially to us. One evening, looking about in a great city, I saw through the window into a large nursery, where the odious gas had not yet been lighted. Round the fire sat a company of the most delightful children I had ever seen. They were waiting patiently for their tea. It was too good an opportunity to be lost. I hurried away, and gathering together twenty of the best Shadows I could find, returned in a few moments; and entering the nursery, we danced on the walls one of our best dances. To be sure it was mostly extemporized; but I managed to keep it in harmony by singing this song, which I made as we went on. Of course the children could not hear it; they only saw the motions that answered to it; but with them they seemed to be very much delighted indeed, as I shall presently prove to you. This was the song:—

'Swing, swang, swingle, swuff,

Flicker, flacker, fling, fluff!

Thus we go,

To and fro;

Here and there,

Everywhere,

Born and bred;

Never dead,

Only gone.

'On! Come on.

Looming, glooming,

Spreading, fuming,

Shattering, scattering,

Parting, darting,

Settling, starting,

All our life

Is a strife,

And a wearying for rest

On the darkness' friendly breast.

'Joining, splitting,

Rising, sitting,

Laughing, shaking,

Sides all aching,

Grumbling, grim, and gruff.

Swingle, swangle, swuff!

'Now a knot of darkness;

Now dissolved gloom;

Now a pall of blackness

Hiding all the room.

Flicker, flacker, fluff!

Black, and black enough!

'Dancing now like demons;

  Lying like the dead;

  Gladly would we stop it,

    And go down to bed!

But our work we still must do,

Shadow men, as well as you.

'Rooting, rising, shooting,

  Heaving, sinking, creeping;

Hid in corners crooning;

  Splitting, poking, leaping,

Gathering, towering, swooning.

  When we're lurking,

  Yet we're working,

For our labour we must do,

Shadow men, as well as you.

Flicker, flacker, fling, fluff!

Swing, swang, swingle, swuff!'

"'How thick the Shadows are!' said one of the children—a thoughtful little girl.

"'I wonder where they come from,' said a dreamy little boy.

"'I think they grow out of the wall,' answered the little girl; 'for I have been watching them come; first one and then another, and then a whole lot of them. I am sure they grow out of the walls.'

"'Perhaps they have papas and mammas,' said an older boy, with a smile.

"'Yes, yes; and the doctor brings them in his pocket,' said another, a consequential little maiden.

"'No; I'll tell you,' said the older boy: 'they're ghosts.'

"'But ghosts are white.'

"'Oh! but these have got black coming down the chimney.'

"'No,' said a curious-looking, white-faced boy of fourteen, who had been reading by the firelight, and had stopped to hear the little ones talk; 'they're body ghosts; they're not soul ghosts.'

"'A silence followed, broken by the first, the dreamy-eyed boy, who said,—

"'I hope they didn't make me;' at which they all burst out laughing. Just then the nurse brought in their tea, and when she proceeded to light the gas, we vanished."

"I stopped a murder," cried another.

"How? How? How?"

"I will tell you. I had been lurking about a sick-room for some time, where a miser lay, apparently dying. I did not like the place at all, but I felt as if I should be wanted there. There were plenty of lurking-places about, for the room was full of all sorts of old furniture, especially cabinets, chests, and presses. I believe he had in that room every bit of the property he had spent a long life in gathering. I found that he had gold and gold in those places; for one night, when his nurse was away, he crept out of bed, mumbling and shaking, and managed to open one of his chests, though he nearly fell down with the effort. I was peeping over his shoulder, and such a gleam of gold fell upon me, that it nearly killed me. But hearing his nurse coming, he slammed the lid down, and I recovered.

"I tried very hard, but I could not do him any good. For although I made all sorts of shapes on the walls and ceiling, representing evil deeds that he had done, of which there were plenty to choose from, I could make no shapes on his brain or conscience. He had no eyes for anything but gold. And it so happened that his nurse had neither eyes nor heart for anything else either.

"'One day, as she was seated beside his bed, but where he could not see her, stirring some gruel in a basin, to cool it from him, I saw her take a little phial from her bosom, and I knew by the expression of her face both what it was and what she was going to do with it. Fortunately the cork was a little hard to get out, and this gave me one moment to think.

"The room was so crowded with all sorts of things, that although there were no curtains on the four-post bed to hide from the miser the sight of his precious treasures, there was yet but one small part of the ceiling suitable for casting myself upon in the shape I wished to assume. And this spot was hard to reach. But having discovered that upon this very place lay a dull gleam of firelight thrown from a strange old dusty mirror that stood away in some corner, I got in front of the fire, spied where the mirror was, threw myself upon it, and bounded from its face upon the oval pool of dim light on the ceiling, assuming, as I passed, the shape of an old stooping hag, who poured something from a phial into a basin. I made the handle of the spoon with my own nose, ha! ha!" And the shadow-hand caressed the shadow-tip of the shadow-nose, before the shadow-tongue resumed.

"The old miser saw me: he would not taste the gruel that night, although his nurse coaxed and scolded till they were both weary. She pretended to taste it herself, and to think it very good; but at last retired into a corner, and after making as if she were eating it, took good care to pour it all out into the ashes."

"But she must either succeed, or starve him, at last," interposed a Shadow.

"I will tell you."

"And," interposed a third, "he was not worth saving."

"He might repent," suggested another who was more benevolent.

"No chance of that," returned the former. "Misers never do. The love of money has less in it to cure itself than any other wickedness into which wretched men can fall. What a mercy it is to be born a Shadow! Wickedness does not stick to us. What do we care for gold!—Rubbish!"

"Amen! Amen! Amen!" came from a hundred shadow-voices.

"You should have let her murder him, and so you would have been quit of him."

"And besides, how was he to escape at last? He could never get rid of her, you know."

"I was going to tell you," resumed the narrator, "only you had so many shadow-remarks to make, that you would not let me."

"Go on; go on."

"There was a little grandchild who used to come and see him sometimes—the only creature the miser cared for. Her mother was his daughter; but the old man would never see her, because she had married against his will. Her husband was now dead, but he had not forgiven her yet. After the shadow he had seen, however, he said to himself, as he lay awake that night—I saw the words on his face—'How shall I get rid of that old devil? If I don't eat I shall die; and if I do eat I shall be poisoned. I wish little Mary would come. Ah! her mother would never have served me so.' He lay awake, thinking such things over and over again, all night long, and I stood watching him from a dark corner, till the dayspring came and shook me out. When I came back next night, the room was tidy and clean. His own daughter, a sad-faced but beautiful woman, sat by his bedside; and little Mary was curled up on the floor by the fire, imitating us, by making queer shadows on the ceiling with her twisted hands. But she could not think how ever they got there. And no wonder, for I helped her to some very unaccountable ones."

"I have a story about a granddaughter, too," said another, the moment that speaker ceased.

"Tell it. Tell it."

"Last Christmas-day," he began, "I and a troop of us set out in the twilight to find some house where we could all have something to do; for we had made up our minds to act together. We tried several, but found objections to them all. At last we espied a large lonely country-house, and hastening to it, we found great preparations making for the Christmas dinner. We rushed into it, scampered all over it, and made up our minds in a moment that it would do. We amused ourselves in the nursery first, where there were several children being dressed for dinner. We generally do go to the nursery first, your majesty. This time we were especially charmed with a little girl about five years old, who clapped her hands and danced about with delight at the antics we performed; and we said we would do something for her if we had a chance. The company began to arrive; and at every arrival we rushed to the hall, and cut wonderful capers of welcome. Between times we scudded away to see how the dressing went on. One girl about eighteen was delightful. She dressed herself as if she did not care much about it, but could not help doing it prettily. When she took her last look at the phantom in the glass, she half smiled to it.—But we do not like those creatures that come into the mirrors at all, your majesty. We don't understand them. They are dreadful to us.— She looked rather sad and pale, but very sweet and hopeful. So we wanted to know all about her, and soon found out that she was a distant relation and a great favourite of the gentleman of the house, an old man, in whose face benevolence was mingled with obstinacy and a deep shade of the tyrannical. We could not admire him much; but we would not make up our minds all at once: Shadows never do.

"The dinner-bell rang, and down we hurried. The children all looked happy, and we were merry. But there was one cross fellow among the servants, and didn't we plague him! and didn't we get fun out of him! When he was bringing up dishes, we lay in wait for him at every corner, and sprang upon him from the floor, and from over the banisters, and down from the cornices. He started and stumbled and blundered so in consequence, that his fellow-servants thought he was tipsy. Once he dropped a plate, and had to pick up the pieces, and hurry away with them; and didn't we pursue him as he went! It was lucky for him his master did not see how he went on; but we took care not to let him get into any real scrape, though he was quite dazed with the dodging of the unaccountable shadows. Sometimes he thought the walls were coming down upon him; sometimes that the floor was gaping to swallow him; sometimes that he would be knocked to pieces by the hurrying to and fro, or be smothered in the black crowd.

"When the blazing plum-pudding was carried in we made a perfect shadow-carnival about it, dancing and mumming in the blue flames, like mad demons. And how the children screamed with delight!

"The old gentleman, who was very fond of children, was laughing his heartiest laugh, when a loud knock came to the hall-door. The fair maiden started, turned paler, and then red as the Christmas fire. I saw it, and flung my hands across her face. She was very glad, and I know she said in her heart, 'You kind Shadow!' which paid me well. Then I followed the rest into the hall, and found there a jolly, handsome, brown-faced sailor, evidently a son of the house. The old man received him with tears in his eyes, and the children with shouts of joy. The maiden escaped in the confusion, just in time to save herself from fainting. We crowded about the lamp to hide her retreat, and nearly put it out; and the butler could not get it to burn up before she had glided into her place again, relieved to find the room so dark. The sailor only had seen her go, and now he sat down beside her, and, without a word, got hold of her hand in the gloom. When we all scattered to the walls and the corners, and the lamp blazed up again, he let her hand go.

"During the rest of the dinner the old man watched the two, and saw that there was something between them, and was very angry. For he was an important man in his own estimation, and they had never consulted him. The fact was, they had never known their own minds till the sailor had gone upon his last voyage, and had learned each other's only this moment.—We found out all this by watching them, and then talking together about it afterwards.—The old gentleman saw, too, that his favourite, who was under such obligation to him for loving her so much, loved his son better than him; and he grew by degrees so jealous that he overshadowed the whole table with his morose looks and short answers. That kind of shadowing is very different from ours; and the Christmas dessert grew so gloomy that we Shadows could not bear it, and were delighted when the ladies rose to go to the drawing-room. The gentlemen would not stay behind the ladies, even for the sake of the well-known wine. So the moody host, notwithstanding his hospitality, was left alone at the table in the great silent room. We followed the company upstairs to the drawing-room, and thence to the nursery for snap-dragon; but while they were busy with this most shadowy of games, nearly all the Shadows crept downstairs again to the dining-room, where the old man still sat, gnawing the bone of his own selfishness. They crowded into the room, and by using every kind of expansion—blowing themselves out like soap-bubbles—they succeeded in heaping up the whole room with shade upon shade. They clustered thickest about the fire and the lamp, till at last they almost drowned them in hills of darkness.

"Before they had accomplished so much, the children, tired with fun and frolic, had been put to bed. But the little girl of five years old, with whom we had been so pleased when first we arrived, could not go to sleep. She had a little room of her own; and I had watched her to bed, and now kept her awake by gambolling in the rays of the night-light. When her eyes were once fixed upon me, I took the shape of her grandfather, representing him on the wall as he sat in his chair, with his head bent down and his arms hanging listlessly by his sides. And the child remembered that that was just as she had seen him last; for she had happened to peep in at the dining-room door after all the rest had gone upstairs. 'What if he should be sitting there still,' thought she, 'all alone in the dark!' She scrambled out of bed and crept down.

"Meantime the others had made the room below so dark, that only the face and white hair of the old man could be dimly discerned in the shadowy crowd. For he had filled his own mind with shadows, which we Shadows wanted to draw out of him. Those shadows are very different from us, your majesty knows. He was thinking of all the disappointments he had had in life, and of all the ingratitude he had met with. And he thought far more of the good he had done, than the good others had got. 'After all I have done for them,' said he, with a sigh of bitterness, 'not one of them cares a straw for me. My own children will be glad when I am gone!'—At that instant he lifted up his eyes and saw, standing close by the door, a tiny figure in a long nightgown. The door behind her was shut. It was my little friend, who had crept in noiselessly. A pang of icy fear shot to the old man's heart, but it melted away as fast, for we made a lane through us for a single ray from the fire to fall on the face of the little sprite; and he thought it was a child of his own that had died when just the age of her child-niece, who now stood looking for her grandfather among the Shadows. He thought she had come out of her grave in the cold darkness to ask why her father was sitting alone on Christmas-day. And he felt he had no answer to give his little ghost, but one he would be ashamed for her to hear. But his grandchild saw him now, and walked up to him with a childish stateliness, stumbling once or twice on what seemed her long shroud. Pushing through the crowded shadows, she reached him, climbed upon his knee, laid her little long-haired head on his shoulders, and said,—'Ganpa! you goomy? Isn't it your Kissy-Day too, ganpa?'

"A new fount of love seemed to burst from the clay of the old man's heart. He clasped the child to his bosom, and wept. Then, without a word, he rose with her in his arms, carried her up to her room, and laying her down in her bed, covered her up, kissed her sweet little mouth unconscious of reproof, and then went to the drawing-room.

"As soon as he entered, he saw the culprits in a quiet corner alone. He went up to them, took a hand of each, and joining them in both his, said, 'God bless you!' Then he turned to the rest of the company, and 'Now,' said he, 'let's have a Christmas carol.'—And well he might; for though I have paid many visits to the house, I have never seen him cross since; and I am sure that must cost him a good deal of trouble."

"We have just come from a great palace," said another, "where we knew there were many children, and where we thought to hear glad voices, and see royally merry looks. But as soon as we entered, we became aware that one mighty Shadow shrouded the whole; and that Shadow deepened and deepened, till it gathered in darkness about the reposing form of a wise prince. When we saw him, we could move no more, but clung heavily to the walls, and by our stillness added to the sorrow of the hour. And when we saw the mother of her people weeping with bowed head for the loss of him in whom she had trusted, we were seized with such a longing to be Shadows no more, but winged angels, which are the white shadows cast in heaven from the Light of Light, so as to gather around her, and hover over her with comforting, that we vanished from the walls, and found ourselves floating high above the towers of the palace, where we met the angels on their way, and knew that our service was not needed."

By this time there was a glimmer of approaching moonlight, and the king began to see several of those stranger Shadows, with human faces and eyes, moving about amongst the crowd. He knew at once that they did not belong to his dominion. They looked at him, and came near him, and passed slowly, but they never made any obeisance, or gave sign of homage. And what their eyes said to him, the king only could tell. And he did not tell.

"What are those other Shadows that move through the crowd?" said he to one of his subjects near him.

The Shadow started, looked round, shivered slightly, and laid his finger on his lips. Then leading the king a little aside, and looking carefully about him once more,—

"I do not know," said he in a low tone, "what they are. I have heard of them often, but only once did I ever see any of them before. That was when some of us one night paid a visit to a man who sat much alone, and was said to think a great deal. We saw two of those sitting in the room with him, and he was as pale as they were. We could not cross the threshold, but shivered and shook, and felt ready to melt away. Is not your majesty afraid of them too?"

But the king made no answer; and before he could speak again, the moon had climbed above the mighty pillars of the church of the Shadows, and looked in at the great window of the sky.

The shapes had all vanished; and the king, again lifting up his eyes, saw but the wall of his own chamber, on which flickered the Shadow of a Little Child. He looked down, and there, sitting on a stool by the fire, he saw one of his own little ones, waiting to say good-night to his father, and go to bed early, that he might rise early too, and be very good and happy all Christmas-day.

And Ralph Rinkelmann rejoiced that he was a man, and not a Shadow.

But as the Shadows vanished they left the sense of song in the king's brain. And the words of their song must have been something like these:—

"Shadows, Shadows, Shadows all!

Shadow birth and funeral!

Shadow moons gleam overhead;

Over shadow-graves we tread.

Shadow-hope lives, grows, and dies.

Shadow-love from shadow-eyes

Shadow-ward entices on

To shadow-words on shadow-stone,

Closing up the shadow-tale

With a shadow-shadow-wail.

"Shadow-man, thou art a gloom

Cast upon a shadow-tomb

Through the endless shadow air,

From the shadow sitting there,

On a moveless shadow-throne,

Glooming through the ages gone;

North and south, and in and out,

East and west, and all about,

Flinging Shadows everywhere

On the shadow-painted air

Shadow-man, thou hast no story;

Nothing but a shadow-glory."

But Ralph Rinkelmann said to himself,—

"They are but Shadows that sing thus; for a Shadow can see but Shadows. A man sees a man where a Shadow sees only a Shadow."

And he was comforted in himself.

About Author

Elizabeth Yates wrote of Sir Gibbie, "It moved me the way books did when, as a child, the great gates of literature began to open and first encounters with noble thoughts and utterances were unspeakably thrilling."

Even Mark Twain, who initially disliked MacDonald, became friends with him, and there is some evidence that Twain was influenced by him. The Christian author Oswald Chambers wrote in his "Christian Disciplines" that "it is a striking indication of the trend and shallowness of the modern reading public that George MacDonald's books have been so neglected".

Early life

George MacDonald was born on 10 December 1824 at Huntly, Aberdeenshire, Scotland. His father, a farmer, was one of the MacDonalds of Glen Coe and a direct descendant of one of the families that suffered in the massacre of 1692.

MacDonald grew up in an unusually literate environment: one of his maternal uncles was a notable Celtic scholar, editor of the Gaelic Highland Dictionary and collector of fairy tales and Celtic poetry. His paternal grandfather had supported the publication of an Ossian edition, the controversial Celtic text believed by some to have contributed to the starting of European Romanticism. MacDonald's step-uncle was a Shakespeare scholar, and his paternal cousin another Celtic academic. Both his parents were readers, his father harbouring predilections for Newton, Burns, Cowper, Chalmers, Coleridge, and Darwin, to quote a few, while his mother had received a classical education which included multiple languages.

An account cited how the young George suffered lapses in health in his early years and was subject to problems with his lungs such as asthma, bronchitis and even a bout of tuberculosis. This last illness was considered a family disease and two of MacDonald's brothers, his mother, and later three of his own children actually died from the ailment. Even in his adult life, he was constantly travelling in search of purer air for his lungs.

MacDonald grew up in the Congregational Church, with an atmosphere of Calvinism. However, his family was atypical, with his paternal grandfather a Catholic-born, fiddle-playing, Presbyterian elder; his paternal grandmother an Independent church rebel; his mother was a sister to the Gallic-speaking radical who became moderator of the disrupting Free Church, while his step-mother, to whom he was also very close, was the daughter of a Scottish Episcopalian priest.

MacDonald graduated from the University of Aberdeen in 1845 with a master's degree in chemistry and physics. He spent the next several years struggling with matters of faith and deciding what to do with his life. His son, biographer Greville MacDonald stated that his father could have pursued a career in the medical field but he speculated that lack of money put an end to this prospect. It was only in 1848 when MacDonald began theological training at Highbury College for the Congregational ministry.

Early career

MacDonald was appointed minister of Trinity Congregational Church, Arundel, in 1850, after briefly serving as a locum minister in Ireland. However, his sermons—which preached God's universal love and that everyone was capable of redemption —met with little favour and his salary was cut in half. In May 1853, MacDonald tendered his resignation from his pastoral duties at Arundel. Later he was engaged in ministerial work in Manchester, leaving that because of poor health. An account cited the role of Lady Byron in convincing MacDonald to travel to Algiers in 1856 with the hope that the sojourn would help turn his health around. When he got back, he settled in London and taught for some time at the University of London. MacDonald was also for a time editor of Good Words for the Young.

Writing Career

MacDonald's first novel David Elginbrod was published in 1863.

George MacDonald is often regarded as the founding father of modern fantasy writing. George MacDonald's best-known works are Phantastes, The Princess and the Goblin, At the Back of the North Wind, and Lilith (1895), all fantasy novels, and fairy tales such as "The Light Princess", "The Golden Key", and "The Wise Woman". "I write, not for children," he wrote, "but for the child-like, whether they be of five, or fifty, or seventy-five." MacDonald also published some volumes of sermons, the pulpit not having proved an unreservedly successful venue.

After his literary success, MacDonald went on to do a lecture tour in the United States in 1872–1873, after being invited to do so by a lecture company, the Boston Lyceum Bureau. On the tour, MacDonald lectured about other poets such as Robert Burns, Shakespeare, and Tom Hood. He performed this lecture to great acclaim, speaking in Boston to crowds in the neighborhood of three thousand people.

MacDonald served as a mentor to Lewis Carroll (the pen-name of Charles Lutwidge Dodgson); it was MacDonald's advice, and the enthusiastic reception of Alice by MacDonald's many sons and daughters, that convinced Carroll to submit Alice for publication. Carroll, one of the finest Victorian photographers, also created photographic portraits of several of the MacDonald children. MacDonald was also friends with John Ruskin, and served as a go-between in Ruskin's long courtship with Rose La Touche. While in America he was befriended by Longfellow and Walt Whitman.

MacDonald's use of fantasy as a literary medium for exploring the human condition greatly influenced a generation of notable authors, including C. S. Lewis, who featured him as a character in his The Great Divorce. In his introduction to his MacDonald anthology, Lewis speaks highly of MacDonald's views:

This collection, as I have said, was designed not to revive MacDonald's literary reputation but to spread his religious teaching. Hence most of my extracts are taken from the three volumes of Unspoken Sermons. My own debt to this book is almost as great as one man can owe to another: and nearly all serious inquirers to whom I have introduced it acknowledge that it has given them great help—sometimes indispensable help toward the very acceptance of the Christian faith. ...

I know hardly any other writer who seems to be closer, or more continually close, to the Spirit of Christ Himself. Hence his Christ-like union of tenderness and severity. Nowhere else outside the New Testament have I found terror and comfort so intertwined. ...

In making this collection I was discharging a debt of justice. I have never concealed the fact that I regarded him as my master; indeed I fancy I have never written a book in which I did not quote from him. But it has not seemed to me that those who have received my books kindly take even now sufficient notice of the affiliation. Honesty drives me to emphasize it.

Others he influenced include J. R. R. Tolkien and Madeleine L'Engle. MacDonald's non-fantasy novels, such as Alec Forbes, had their influence as well; they were among the first realistic Scottish novels, and as such MacDonald has been credited with founding the "kailyard school" of Scottish writing.

Chesterton cited The Princess and the Goblin as a book that had "made a difference to my whole existence", in showing "how near both the best and the worst things are to us from the first... and making all the ordinary staircases and doors and windows into magical things."

Later life

In 1877 he was given a civil list pension. From 1879 he and his family moved to Bordighera, in a place much loved by British expatriates, the Riviera dei Fiori in Liguria, Italy, almost on the French border. In that locality there also was an Anglican church, All Saints, which he attended. Deeply enamoured of the Riviera, he spent 20 years there, writing almost half of his whole literary production, especially the fantasy work. MacDonald founded a literary studio in that Ligurian town, naming it Casa Coraggio (Bravery House). It soon became one of the most renowned cultural centres of that period, well attended by British and Italian travellers, and by locals, with presentations of classic plays and readings of Dante and Shakespeare often being held.

In 1900 he moved into St George's Wood, Haslemere, a house designed for him by his son, Robert, its building overseen by his eldest son, Greville.

George MacDonald died on 18 September 1905 in Ashtead, Surrey, England. He was cremated in Woking, Surrey, England and his ashes were buried in Bordighera, in the English cemetery, along with his wife Louisa and daughters Lilia and Grace.

Personal life

MacDonald married Louisa Powell in Hackney in 1851, with whom he raised a family of eleven children: Lilia Scott (1852), Mary Josephine (1853-1878), Caroline Grace (1854), Greville Matheson (1856-1944), Irene (1857), Winifred Louise (1858), Ronald (1860–1933), Robert Falconer (1862–1913), Maurice (1864), Bernard Powell (1865–1928), and George Mackay (1867–1909?).

His son Greville became a noted medical specialist, a pioneer of the Peasant Arts movement, wrote numerous fairy tales for children, and ensured that new editions of his father's works were published. Another son, Ronald, became a novelist. His daughter Mary was engaged to the artist Edward Robert Hughes until her death in 1878. Ronald's son, Philip MacDonald (George MacDonald's grandson), became a Hollywood screenwriter.

Tuberculosis caused the death of several family members, including Lilia, Mary Josephine, Grace, Maurice as well as one granddaughter and a daughter-in-law. MacDonald was said to have been particularly affected by the death of Lilia, her eldest.

Theology

According to biographer William Raeper, MacDonald's theology "celebrated the rediscovery of God as Father, and sought to encourage an intuitive response to God and Christ through quickening his readers' spirits in their reading of the Bible and their perception of nature."

MacDonald's oft-mentioned universalism is not the idea that everyone will automatically be saved, but is closer to Gregory of Nyssa in the view that all will ultimately repent and be restored to God.

MacDonald appears to have never felt comfortable with some aspects of Calvinist doctrine, feeling that its principles were inherently "unfair"; when the doctrine of predestination was first explained to him, he burst into tears (although assured that he was one of the elect). Later novels, such as Robert Falconer and Lilith, show a distaste for the idea that God's electing love is limited to some and denied to others.

Chesterton noted that only a man who had "escaped" Calvinism could say that God is easy to please and hard to satisfy.

MacDonald rejected the doctrine of penal substitutionary atonement as developed by John Calvin, which argues that Christ has taken the place of sinners and is punished by the wrath of God in their place, believing that in turn it raised serious questions about the character and nature of God. Instead, he taught that Christ had come to save people from their sins, and not from a Divine penalty for their sins: the problem was not the need to appease a wrathful God, but the disease of cosmic evil itself. MacDonald frequently described the atonement in terms similar to the Christus Victor theory. MacDonald posed the rhetorical question, "Did he not foil and slay evil by letting all the waves and billows of its horrid sea break upon him, go over him, and die without rebound—spend their rage, fall defeated, and cease? Verily, he made atonement!"

MacDonald was convinced that God does not punish except to amend, and that the sole end of His greatest anger is the amelioration of the guilty. As the doctor uses fire and steel in certain deep-seated diseases, so God may use hell-fire if necessary to heal the hardened sinner. MacDonald declared, "I believe that no hell will be lacking which would help the just mercy of God to redeem his children." MacDonald posed the rhetorical question, "When we say that God is Love, do we teach men that their fear of Him is groundless?" He replied, "No. As much as they were will come upon them, possibly far more. ... The wrath will consume what they call themselves; so that the selves God made shall appear."

However, true repentance, in the sense of freely chosen moral growth, is essential to this process, and, in MacDonald's optimistic view, inevitable for all beings (see universal reconciliation).

MacDonald states his theological views most distinctly in the sermon "Justice", found in the third volume of Unspoken Sermons. (Source: Wikipedia)